Also by Stephen King

STEPHEN KING

THE BODY

SCRIBNER

New York   London   Toronto   Sydney   New Delhi

Scribner
An Imprint of Simon & Schuster, Inc.
1230 Avenue of the Americas
New York, NY 10020

This story was previously published in *Different Seasons*
copyright © 1982 by Stephen King

First Scribner trade paperback edition June 2018

SCRIBNER and design are registered trademarks of The Gale Group, Inc., used under license by Simon & Schuster, Inc., the publisher of this work.

For information about special discounts for bulk purchases, please contact Simon & Schuster Special Sales at 1-866-506-1949 or business@simonandschuster.com

The Simon & Schuster Speakers Bureau can bring authors to your live event. For more information or to book an event, contact the Simon & Schuster Speakers Bureau at 1-866-248-3049 or visit our website at www.simonspeakers.com.

Interior design by Erich Hobbing

Manufactured in the United States of America

9   10

Library of Congress Cataloging-in-Publication Data is available.

ISBN 978-1-9821-0353-8
ISBN 978-1-9821-0559-4 (ebook)

Permissions acknowledgments appear on page 181.

For George McLeod

THE BODY

1

The most important things are the hardest things to say. They are the things you get ashamed of, because words diminish them—words shrink things that seemed limitless when they were in your head to no more than living size when they're brought out. But it's more than that, isn't it? The most important things lie too close to wherever your secret heart is buried, like landmarks to a treasure your enemies would love to steal away. And you may make revelations that cost you dearly only to have people look at you in a funny way, not understanding what you've said at all, or why you thought it was so important that you almost cried while you were saying it. That's the worst, I think. When the secret stays locked within not for want of a teller but for want of an understanding ear.

I was twelve going on thirteen when I first saw a dead human being. It happened in 1960, a long time ago . . . although sometimes it doesn't seem that long to me. Especially on the nights I wake up from dreams where the hail falls into his open eyes.

2

We had a treehouse in a big elm which overhung a vacant lot in Castle Rock. There's a moving company on that lot today, and the elm is gone. Progress. It was a sort of social club, although it had no name. There were five, maybe six steady guys and some other wet ends who just hung around. We'd let them come up when there was a card game and we needed some fresh blood. The game was usually blackjack and we played for pennies, nickel limit. But you got double money on blackjack and five-card-under . . . *triple* money on six-card-under, although Teddy was the only guy crazy enough to go for that.

The sides of the treehouse were planks scavenged from the shitpile behind Mackey Lumber & Building Supply on Carbine Road—they were splintery and full of knotholes we plugged with either toilet paper or paper towels. The roof was a corrugated tin sheet we hawked from the dump, looking over our shoulders all the time we were hustling it out of there, because the dump custodian's dog was supposed to be a real kid-eating monster. We found a screen door out there on the same day. It was flyproof but really rusty—I mean, that rust was *extreme*. No matter what time of day you looked out that screen door, it looked like sunset.

Besides playing cards, the club was a good place to go and smoke cigarettes and look at girly books. There were half a dozen battered tin ashtrays that said camels on the bottom, a lot of centerfolds tacked to the splintery walls, twenty or thirty dog-eared packs of Bike cards (Teddy got them from his uncle, who ran the Castle Rock Stationery Shoppe—when Teddy's unc asked him one day what kind of cards we played, Teddy said we had cribbage tournaments and Teddy's unc thought that was just fine), a set of plastic poker chips, and a pile of ancient *Master Detective* murder magazines to leaf through if there was nothing else shaking. We also built a 12" x 10" secret compartment under the floor to hide most of this stuff in on the rare occasions when some kid's father decided it was time to do the we're-really-good-pals routine. When it rained, being in the club was like being inside a Jamaican steel drum . . . but that summer there had been no rain.

It had been the driest and hottest since 1907—or so the newspapers said, and on that Friday preceding the Labor Day weekend and the start of another school year, even the golden-rod in the fields and the ditches beside the backroads looked parched and poorly. Nobody's garden had done doodly-squat that year, and the big displays of canning stuff in the Castle Rock Red & White were still there, gathering dust. No one had anything to put up that summer, except maybe dandelion wine.

Teddy and Chris and I were up in the club on that Friday morning, glooming to each other about school being so near and playing cards and swapping the same old traveling sales-man jokes and frenchman jokes. How do you know when a frenchman's been in your back yard? Well, your garbage cans are empty and your dog is pregnant. Teddy would try to look offended, but he was the first one to bring in a joke as soon as he heard it, only switching frenchman to polack.

The elm gave good shade, but we already had our shirts off so we wouldn't sweat them up too bad. We were playing three-penny-scat, the dullest card-game ever invented, but it was too hot to think about anything more complicated. We'd had a pretty fair scratch ballteam until the middle of August and then a lot of kids just drifted away. Too hot.

I was down to my ride and building spades. I'd started with thirteen, gotten an eight to make twenty-one, and nothing had happened since then. Chris knocked. I took my last draw and got nothing helpful.

"Twenty-nine," Chris said, laying down diamonds.

"Twenty-two," Teddy said, looking disgusted.

"Piss up a rope," I said, and tossed my cards onto the table face down.

"Gordie's out, ole Gordie just bit the bag and stepped out

the door," Teddy bugled, and then gave out with his patented Teddy Duchamp laugh—*Eeee-eee-eee,* like a rusty nail being slowly hauled out of a rotten board. Well, he was weird; we all knew it. He was close to being thirteen like the rest of us, but the thick glasses and the hearing aid he wore sometimes made him look like an old man. Kids were always trying to cadge smokes off him on the street, but the bugle in his shirt was just his hearing-aid battery.

In spite of the glasses and the flesh-colored button always screwed into his ear, Teddy couldn't see very well and often misunderstood the things people said to him. In baseball you had to have him play the fences, way beyond Chris in left field and Billy Greer in right. You just hoped no one would hit one that far because Teddy would go grimly after it, see it or not. Every now and then he got bonked a good one, and once he went out cold when he ran full-tilt-boogie into the fence by the treehouse. He lay there on his back with his eyes showing whites for almost five minutes, and I got scared. Then he woke up and walked around with a bloody nose and a huge purple lump rising on his forehead, trying to claim that the ball was foul.

His eyesight was just naturally bad, but there was nothing natural about what had happened to his ears. Back in those days, when it was cool to get your hair cut so that your ears stuck out like a couple of jug-handles, Teddy had Castle Rock's first Beatle haircut—four years before anyone in America had ever heard of the Beatles. He kept his ears covered because they looked like two lumps of warm wax.

One day when he was eight, Teddy's father got pissed at him for breaking a plate. His mother was working at the shoe factory in South Paris when it happened and by the time she found out about it, it was all over.

Teddy's dad took Teddy over to the big woodstove at the back of the kitchen and shoved the side of Teddy's head down against one of the cast-iron burner plates. He held it down there for about ten seconds. Then he yanked Teddy up by the hair of the head and did the other side. Then he called the Central Main General Emergency unit and told them to come get his boy. Then he hung up the phone, went into the closet, got his .410, and sat down to watch the daytime stories on TV with the shotgun laid across his knees. When Mrs. Burroughs from next door came over to ask if Teddy was all right—she'd heard the screaming—Teddy's dad pointed the shotgun at her. Mrs. Burroughs went out of the Duchamp house at roughly the speed of light, locked herself into her own house, and called the police. When the ambulance came, Mr. Duchamp let the orderlies in and then went out on the back porch to stand guard while they wheeled Teddy to the old portholed Buick ambulance on a stretcher.

Teddy's dad explained to the orderlies that while the fucking brass hats said the area was clear, there were still kraut snipers everywhere. One of the orderlies asked Teddy's dad if he thought he could hold on. Teddy's dad smiled tightly and told the orderly he'd hold until hell was a Frigidaire dealership, if that's what it took. The orderly saluted, and Teddy's dad snapped it right back at him. A few minutes after the ambulance left, the state police arrived and relieved Norman Duchamp of duty.

He'd been doing odd things like shooting cats and lighting fires in mailboxes for over a year, and after the atrocity he had visited upon his son, they had a quick hearing and sent him to Togus, which is a VA hospital. Togus is where you have to go if you're a section eight. Teddy's dad had stormed the beach at Normandy, and that's just the way Teddy always put it. Teddy was proud of his old man in spite of what his old man had done to him, and Teddy went with his mom to visit him every week.

He was the dumbest guy we hung around with, I guess, and

he was crazy. He'd take the craziest chances you can imagine, and get away with them. His big thing was what he called "truck-dodging." He'd run out in front of them on 196 and sometimes they'd miss him by bare inches. God knew how many heart attacks he'd caused, and he'd be laughing while the windblast from the passing truck rippled his clothes. It scared us because his vision was so lousy, Coke-bottle glasses or not. It seemed like only a matter of time before he misjudged one of those trucks. And you had to be careful what you dared him, because Teddy would do anything on a dare.

"Gordie's out, eeeeee-eee-eee!"

"Screw," I said, and picked up a *Master Detective* to read while they played it out. I turned to "He Stomped the Pretty Co-Ed to Death in a Stalled Elevator" and got right into it.

Teddy picked up his cards, gave them one brief look, and said: "I knock."

"You four-eyed pile of shit!" Chris cried.

"The pile of shit has a thousand eyes," Teddy said gravely, and both Chris and I cracked up. Teddy stared at us with a slight frown, as if wondering what had gotten us laughing. That was another thing about the cat—he was always coming out with weird stuff like "The pile of shit has a thousand eyes," and you could never be sure if he *meant* it to be funny or if it just happened that way. He'd look at the people who were laughing with that slight frown on his face, as if to say: *O Lord what is it this time?*

Teddy had a natural thirty—jack, queen, and king of clubs. Chris had only sixteen and went down to his ride.

Teddy was shuffling the cards in his clumsy way and I was just getting to the gooshy part of the murder story, where this deranged sailor from New Orleans was doing the Bristol Stomp all over this college girl from Bryn Mawr because he couldn't stand being in closed-in places, when we heard some-

one coming fast up the ladder nailed to the side of the elm. A
fist rapped on the underside of the trapdoor.

"Who goes?" Chris yelled.

"Vern!" He sounded excited and out of breath.

I went to the trapdoor and pulled the bolt. The trapdoor
banged up and Vern Tessio, one of the other regulars, pulled
himself into the clubhouse. He was sweating buckets and his
hair, which he usually kept combed in a perfect imitation of
his rock and roll idol, Bobby Rydell, was plastered to his bullet head in chunks and strings.

"Wow, man," he panted. "Wait'll you hear this."

"Hear what?" I asked.

"Lemme get my breath. I ran all the way from my house."

"*I ran all the way home,*" Teddy wavered in a dreadful Little
Anthony falsetto, "*just to say I'm soh-ree—*"

"Fuck your hand, man," Vern said.

"Drop dead in a shed, Fred," Teddy returned smartly.

"You ran all the way from your place?" Chris asked unbe-
lievingly. "Man, you're crazy." Vern's house was two miles
down Grand Street. "It must be ninety out there."

"This is worth it," Vern said. "Holy Jeezum. You won't
believe this. Sincerely." He slapped his sweaty forehead to
show us how sincere he was.

"Okay, what?" Chris asked.

"Can you guys camp out tonight?" Vern was looking at us
earnestly, excitedly. His eyes looked like raisins pushed into
dark circles of sweat. "I mean, if you tell your folks we're gonna
tent out in my back field?"

"Yeah, I guess so," Chris said, picking up his new hand
and looking at it. "But my dad's on a mean streak. Drinkin,
y'know."

"You got to, man," Vern said. "Sincerely. You won't *believe*
this. Can you, Gordie?"

"Probably."

I was able to do most stuff like that—in fact, I'd been like the Invisible Boy that whole summer. In April my older brother, Dennis, had been killed in a Jeep accident. That was at Fort Benning, Georgia, where he was in Basic. He and another guy were on their way to the PX and an Army truck hit them broadside. Dennis was killed instantly and his passenger had been in a coma ever since. Dennis would have been twenty-two later that week. I'd already picked out a birthday card for him at Dahlie's over in Castle Green.

I cried when I heard, and I cried more at the funeral, and I couldn't believe that Dennis was gone, that anyone that used to knuckle my head or scare me with a rubber spider until I cried or give me a kiss when I fell down and scraped both knees bloody and whisper in my ear, "Now stop cryin, ya baby!"— that a person who had *touched* me could be dead. It hurt me and it scared me that he could be dead . . . but it seemed to have taken all the heart out of my parents. For me, Dennis was hardly more than an acquaintance. He was ten years older than me if you can dig it, and he had his own friends and classmates. We ate at the same table for a lot of years, and sometimes he was my friend and sometimes my tormentor, but mostly he was, you know, just a guy. When he died he'd been gone for a year except for a couple of furloughs. We didn't even look alike. It took me a long time after that summer to realize that most of the tears I cried were for my mom and dad. Fat lot of good it did them, or me.

"So what are you pissing and moaning about, Vern-O?" Teddy asked.

"I knock," Chris said.

"*What?*" Teddy screamed, immediately forgetting all about Vern. "You friggin liar! You ain't got no pat hand. I didn't deal you no pat hand."

Chris smirked. "Make your draw, shitheap."

Teddy reached for the top card on the pile of Bikes. Chris reached for the Winstons on the ledge behind him. I bent over to pick up my detective magazine.

Vern Tessio said: "You guys want to go see a dead body?"

Everybody stopped.

3

We'd all heard about it on the radio, of course. The radio, a Philco with a cracked case which had also been scavenged from the dump, played all the time. We kept it tuned to WALM in Lewiston, which churned out the super-hits and the boss oldies: "What in the World's Come Over You" by Jack Scott and "This Time" by Troy Shondell and "King Creole" by Elvis and "Only the Lonely" by Roy Orbison. When the news came on we usually switched some mental dial over to Mute. The news was a lot of happy horseshit about Kennedy and Nixon and Quemoy and Matsu and the missile gap and what a shit that Castro was turning out to be after all. But we had all listened to the Ray Brower story a little more closely, because he was a kid our age.

He was from Chamberlain, a town forty miles or so east of Castle Rock. Three days before Vern came busting into the clubhouse after a two-mile run up Grand Street, Ray Brower had gone out with one of his mother's pots to pick blueberries. When dark came and he still wasn't back, the Browers called the county sheriff and a search started—first just around the kid's house and then spreading to the surrounding towns of Motton and Durham and Pownal. Everybody got into the act—cops, deputies, game wardens, volunteers. But three days later the kid was still missing. You could tell, hearing about

it on the radio, that they were never going to find that poor
sucker alive; eventually the search would just peter away into
nothing. He might have gotten smothered in a gravel pit slide
or drowned in a brook, and ten years from now some hunter
would find his bones. They were already dragging the ponds
in Chamberlain, and the Motton Reservoir.

Nothing like that could happen in southwestern Maine
today; most of the area has become suburbanized, and the bedroom communities surrounding Portland and Lewiston have
spread out like the tentacles of a giant squid. The woods are
still there, and they get heavier as you work your way west
toward the White Mountains, but these days if you can keep
your head long enough to walk five miles in one consistent
direction, you're certain to cross two-lane blacktop. But in
1960 the whole area between Chamberlain and Castle Rock
was undeveloped, and there were places that hadn't even been
logged since before World War II. In those days it was still
possible to walk into the woods and lose your direction there
and die there.

4

Vern Tessio had been under his porch that morning, digging.

We all understood that right away, but maybe I should take
just a minute to explain it to you. Teddy Duchamp was only
about half-bright, but Vern Tessio would never be spending
any of his spare time on *College Bowl* either. Still his brother
Billy was even dumber, as you will see. But first I have to tell
you why Vern was digging under the porch.

Four years ago, when he was eight, Vern buried a quart jar
of pennies under the long Tessio front porch. Vern called the
dark space under the porch his "cave." He was playing a pirate

10

sort of game, and the pennies were buried treasure—only if you were playing pirate with Vern, you couldn't call it buried treasure, you had to call it "booty." So he buried the jar of pennies deep, filled in the hole, and covered the fresh dirt with some of the old leaves that had drifted under there over the years. He drew a treasure map which he put up in his room with the rest of his junk. He forgot all about it for a month or so. Then, being low on cash for a movie or something, he remembered the pennies and went to get his map. But his mom had been in to clean two or three times since then, and had collected all the old homework papers and candy wrappers and comic magazines and joke books. She burned them in the stove to start the cook-fire one morning, and Vern's treasure map went right up the kitchen chimney.

Or so he figured it.

He tried to find the spot from memory and dug there. No luck. To the right and the left of that spot. Still no luck. He gave up for the day but had tried off and on ever since. Four years, man. Four *years*. Isn't that a pisser? You didn't know whether to laugh or cry.

It had gotten to be sort of an obsession with him. The Tessio front porch ran the length of the house, probably forty feet long and seven feet wide. He had dug through damn near every inch of that area two, maybe three times and no pennies. The *number* of pennies began to grow in his mind. When it first happened he told Chris and me that there had been maybe three dollars' worth. A year later he was up to five and just lately it was running around ten, more or less, depending on how broke he was.

Every so often we tried to tell him what was so clear to us—that Billy had known about the jar and dug it up himself. Vern refused to believe it, although he hated Billy like the Arabs hate the Jews and probably would have cheerfully voted the death-penalty on his brother for shoplifting, if the opportunity had ever presented itself. He also refused to ask Billy point blank. Probably he was afraid Billy would laugh and say *Course I got them, you stupid pussy, and there was twenty bucks' worth of pennies in that jar and I spent every fuckin cent of it.* Instead, Vern went out and dug for the pennies whenever the spirit moved him (and whenever Billy wasn't around). He always crawled out from under the porch with his jeans dirty and his hair leafy and his hands empty. We ragged him about it something wicked, and his nickname was Penny—Penny Tessio. I think he came up to the club with his news as quick as he did not just to get it out but to show us that some good had finally come of his penny-hunt.

He had been up that morning before anybody, ate his corn-flakes, and was out in the driveway shooting baskets through the old hoop nailed up on the garage, nothing much to do, no one to play Ghost with or anything, and he decided to have another dig for his pennies. He was under the porch when the screen door slammed up above. He froze, not making a sound. If it was his dad, he would crawl out; if it was Billy, he'd stay put until Billy and his j.d. friend Charlie Hogan had taken off.

Two pairs of footsteps crossed the porch, and then Char-lie Hogan himself said in a trembling, crybaby voice: "Jesus Christ, Billy, what are we gonna do?"

Vern said that just hearing Charlie Hogan talk like that—Charlie, who was one of the toughest kids in town—made him prick up his ears. Charlie, after all, hung out with Ace Merrill and Eyeball Chambers, and if you hung out with cats like that, you had to be tough.

"Nuthin," Billy said. "That's all we're gonna do. Nuthin."

"We gotta do *somethin*," Charlie said, and they sat down on the porch close to where Vern was hunkered down. "Didn't you *see* him?"

Vern took a chance and crept a little closer to the steps,

practically slavering. At that point he thought that maybe Billy and Charlie had been really drunked up and had run somebody down. Vern was careful not to crackle any of the old leaves as he moved. If the two of them found out he was under the porch and had overheard them, you could have put what was left of him in a Ken-L Ration dogfood can.

"It's nuthin to us," Billy Tessio said. "The kid's dead so it's nuthin to him, neither. Who gives a fuck if they ever find him? I don't."

"It was that kid they been talkin about on the radio," Charlie said. "It was, sure as shit. Brocker, Brower, Flowers, whatever his name is. Fuckin train must have hit him."

"Yeah," Billy said. Sound of a scratched match. Vern saw it flicked into the gravel driveway and then smelled cigarette smoke. "It sure did. And you puked."

No words, but Vern sensed emotional waves of shame radiating off Charlie Hogan.

"Well, the girls didn't see it," Billy said after awhile. "Lucky break." From the sound, he clapped Charlie on the back to buck him up. "They'd blab it from here to Portland. We tore out of there fast, though. You think they knew there was something wrong?"

"No," Charlie said. "Marie don't like to go down that Back Harlow Road past the cemetery, anyway. She's afraid of ghosts." Then again in that scared crybaby voice: "Jesus, I wish we'd never boosted no car last night! Just gone to the show like we was gonna!"

Charlie and Billy went with a couple of scags named Marie Dougherty and Beverly Thomas; you never saw such gross-looking broads outside of a carnival show—pimples, moustaches, the whole works. Sometimes the four of them— or maybe six or eight if Fuzzy Bracowicz or Ace Merrill were along with their girls—would boost a car from a Lewiston parking lot and go joyriding out into the country with two or three bottles of Wild Irish Rose wine and a six-pack of ginger ale. They'd take the girls parking somewhere in Castle View or Harlow or Shiloh, drink Purple Jesuses, and make out. Then they'd dump the car somewhere near home. Cheap thrills in the monkey-house, as Chris sometimes said. They'd never been caught at it, but Vern kept hoping. He really dug the idea of visiting Billy on Sundays at the reformatory.

"If we told the cops, they'd want to know how we got way the hell out in Harlow," Billy said. "We ain't got no car, neither of us. It's better if we just keep our mouths shut. Then they can't touch us."

"We could make a nonnamus call," Charlie said.

"They trace those fuckin calls," Billy said ominously. "I seen it on *Highway Patrol.* And *Dragnet.*"

"Yeah, right," Charlie said miserably. "Jesus. I wish Ace'd been with us. We could have told the cops we was in his car."

"Well, he wasn't."

"Yeah," Charlie said. He sighed. "I guess you're right." A cigarette butt flicked into the driveway. "We hadda walk up and take a piss by the tracks, didn't we? Couldn't walk the other way, could we? And I got puke on my new P. F. Fliers." His voice sank a little. "Fuckin kid was laid right out, you know it? Didja see that sonofawhore, Billy?"

"I seen him," Billy said, and a second cigarette butt joined the first in the driveway. "Let's go see if Ace is up. I want some juice."

"We gonna tell him?"

"Charlie, we ain't gonna tell *nobody. Nobody never.* You dig me?"

"I dig you," Charlie said. "Christ Jesus, I wish we never boosted that fucking Dodge."

"Aw, shut the fuck up and come on."

Two pairs of legs clad in tight, wash-faded pegged jeans,

two pairs of feet in black engineer boots with side-buckles, came down the steps. Vern froze on his hands and knees ("My balls crawled up so high I thought they was trine to get back home," he told us), sure his brother would sense him beneath the porch and drag him out and kill him—he and Charlie Hogan would kick the few brains the good Lord had seen fit to give him right out his jug ears and then stomp him with their engineer boots. But they just kept going and when Vern was sure they were really gone, he had crawled out from under the porch and ran here.

5

"You're really lucky," I said. "They *would* have killed you."

Teddy said, "I know the Back Harlow Road. It comes to a dead end by the river. We used to fish for cossies out there."

Chris nodded. "There used to be a bridge, but there was a flood. A long time ago. Now there's just the train-tracks."

"Could a kid really have gotten all the way from Chamberlain to Harlow?" I asked Chris. "That's twenty or thirty miles."

"I think so. He probably happened on the train-tracks and followed them the whole way. Maybe he thought they'd take him out, or maybe he thought he could flag down a train if he had to. But that's just a freight run now—GS&WM up to Derry and Brownsville—and not many of those anymore. He'd have to've walked all the way to Castle Rock to get out. After dark a train must have finally come along . . . and el smacko."

Chris drove his right fist down against his left palm, making a flat noise. Teddy, a veteran of many close calls dodging the pulp-trucks on 196, looked vaguely pleased. I felt a little sick, imagining that kid so far away from home, scared to death but doggedly following the GS&WM tracks, probably walking on the ties because of the night-noises from the over-hanging trees and bushes . . . maybe even from the culverts underneath the railroad bed. And here comes the train, and maybe the big headlight on the front hypnotized him until it was too late to jump. Or maybe he was just lying there on the tracks in a hunger-faint when the train came along. Either way, any way, Chris had the straight of it: el smacko had been the final result. The kid was dead.

"So anyway, you want to go see it?" Vern asked. He was squirming around like he had to go to the bathroom he was so excited.

We all looked at him for a long second, no one saying anything. Then Chris tossed his cards down and said: "Sure! And I bet you anything we get our pictures in the paper!"

"Huh?" Vern said.

"Yeah?" Teddy said, and grinning his crazy truck-dodging grin.

"Look," Chris said, leaning across the ratty card-table. "We can find the body and report it! We'll be on the news!"

"I dunno," Vern said, obviously taken aback. "Billy will know where I found out. He'll beat the living shit outta me."

"No he won't," I said, "because it'll be *us* guys that find that kid, not Billy and Charlie Hogan in a boosted car. Then they won't have to worry about it anymore. They'll probably pin a medal on you, Penny."

"Yeah?" Vern grinned, showing his bad teeth. It was a dazed sort of grin, as if the thought of Billy being pleased with anything he did had acted on him like a hard shot to the chin. "Yeah, you think so?"

Teddy was grinning, too. Then he frowned and said: "Oh-oh."

"What?" Vern asked. He was squirming again, afraid that some really basic objection to the idea had just cropped up in Teddy's mind . . . or what passed for Teddy's mind.

"Our folks," Teddy said. "If we find that kid's body over in South Harlow tomorrow, they're gonna know we didn't spend the night campin out in Vern's back field."

"Yeah," Chris said. "They'll know we went lookin for that kid."

"No they won't," I said. I felt funny—both excited and scared because I knew we could do it and get away with it. The mixture of emotions made me feel heatsick and headachy. I picked up the Bikes to have something to do with my hands and started box-shuffling them. That and how to play cribbage was about all I got for older brother stuff from Dennis. The other kids envied that shuffle, and I guess everyone I knew had asked me to show them how it went . . . everyone except Chris. I guess only Chris knew that showing someone would be like giving away a piece of Dennis, and I just didn't have so much of him that I could afford to pass pieces around.

I said: "We'll just tell em we got bored tenting in Vern's field because we've done it so many times before. So we decided to hike up the tracks and have a campout in the woods. I bet we don't even get hided for it because everybody'll be so excited about what we found."

"My dad'll hide me anyway," Chris said. "He's on a really mean streak this time." He shook his head sullenly. "To hell, it's worth a hiding."

"Okay," Teddy said, getting up. He was still grinning like crazy, ready to break into his high-pitched, cackling laugh at any second. "Let's all get together at Vern's house after lunch. What can we tell em about supper?"

Chris said, "You and me and Gordie can say we're eating at Vern's."

"And I'll tell my mom I'm eating over at Chris's," Vern said.

That would work unless there was some emergency we couldn't control or unless any of the parents got together. And neither Vern's folks or Chris's had a phone. Back then there were a lot of families which still considered a telephone a luxury, especially families of the shirttail variety. And none of us came from the upper crust.

My dad was retired. Vern's dad worked in the mill and was still driving a 1952 DeSoto. Teddy's mom had a house on Danberry Street and she took in a boarder whenever she could get one. She didn't have one that summer; the furnished room to let sign had been up in the parlor window since June. And Chris's dad was always on a "mean streak," more or less; he was a drunk who got welfare off and on—mostly on—and spent most of his time hanging out in Sukey's Tavern with Junior Merrill, Ace Merrill's old man, and a couple of other local rumpots.

Chris didn't talk much about his dad, but we all knew he hated him like poison. Chris was marked up every two weeks or so, bruises on his cheeks and neck or one eye swelled up and as colorful as a sunset, and once he came into school with a big clumsy bandage on the back of his head. Other times he never got to school at all. His mom would call him in sick because he was too lamed up to come in. Chris was smart, really smart, but he played truant a lot, and Mr. Halliburton, the town truant officer, was always showing up at Chris's house, driving his old black Chevrolet with the NO RIDERS sticker in the corner of the windshield. If Chris was being truant and Bertie (as we called him—always behind his back, of course) caught him, he would haul him back to school and see that Chris got detention for a week. But if Bertie found out that Chris was home because his father had beaten the shit out of him, Bertie just went away and didn't say boo to a cuckoo-bird. It never occurred to me to question this set of priorities until about twenty years later.

The year before, Chris had been suspended from school for

three days. A bunch of milk-money disappeared when it was Chris's turn to be room-monitor and collect it, and because he was a Chambers from those no-account Chamberses, he had to take a hike even though he always swore he never hawked that money. That was the time Mr. Chambers put Chris in the hospital for an overnight stay; when his dad heard Chris was suspended, he broke Chris's nose and his right wrist. Chris came from a bad family, all right, and everybody thought he would turn out bad . . . including Chris. His brothers had lived up to the town's expectations admirably. Frank, the eldest, ran away from home when he was seventeen, joined the Navy, and ended up doing a long stretch in Portsmouth for rape and criminal assault. The next-eldest, Richard (his right eye was all funny and jittery, which was why everybody called him Eyeball), had dropped out of high school in the tenth grade, and chummed around with Charlie and Billy Tessio and their j.d. buddies.

"I think all that'll work," I told Chris. "What about John and Marty?" John and Marty DeSpain were two other members of our regular gang.

'They're still away," Chris said. "They won't be back until Monday."

"Oh. That's too bad."

"So are we set?" Vern asked, still squirming. He didn't want the conversation sidetracked even for a minute.

"I guess we are," Chris said. "Who wants to play some more scat?"

No one did. We were too excited to play cards. We climbed down from the treehouse, climbed the fence into the vacant lot, and played three-flies-six-grounders for awhile with Vern's old friction-taped baseball, but that was no fun, either. All we could think about was that kid Brower, hit by a train, and how we were going to see him, or what was left of him. Around ten o'clock we all drifted away home to fix it with our parents.

6

I got to my house at quarter of eleven, after stopping at the drugstore to check out the paperbacks. I did that every couple of days to see if there were any new John D. MacDonalds. I had a quarter and I figured if there was, I'd take it along. But there were only the old ones, and I'd read most of those half a dozen times.

When I got home the car was gone and I remembered that my mom and some of her hen-party friends had gone to Boston to see a concert. A great old concert-goer, my mother. And why not? Her only kid was dead and she had to do something to take her mind off it. I guess that sounds pretty bitter. And I guess if you'd been there, you'd understand why I felt that way.

Dad was out back, passing a fine spray from the hose over his ruined garden. If you couldn't tell it was a lost cause from his glum face, you sure could by looking at the garden itself. The soil was a light, powdery gray. Everything in it was dead except for the corn, which had never grown so much as a single edible ear. Dad said he'd never known how to water a garden; it had to be mother nature or nobody. He'd water too long in one spot and drown the plants. In the next row, plants were dying of thirst. He could never hit a happy medium. But he didn't talk about it often. He'd lost a son in April and a garden in August. And if he didn't want to talk about either one, I guess that was his privilege. It just bugged me that he'd given up talking about everything else, too. That was taking democracy too fucking far.

"Hi, Daddy," I said, standing beside him. I offered him the Rollos I'd bought at the drugstore. "Want one?"

"Hello, Gordon. No thanks." He kept on flicking the fine spray over the hopeless gray earth.

"Be okay if I camp out in Vern Tessio's back field tonight with some of the guys?"

"What guys?"

"Vern. Teddy Duchamp. Maybe Chris."

I expected him to start right in on Chris—how Chris was bad company, a rotten apple from the bottom of the barrel, a thief, and an apprentice juvenile delinquent.

But he just sighed and said, "I suppose it's okay."

"Great! Thanks!"

I turned to go into the house and check out what was on the boob tube when he stopped me with: "Those are the only people you want to be with, aren't they, Gordon?"

I looked back at him, braced for an argument, but there was no argument in him that morning. It would have been better if there had been, I think. His shoulders were slumped. His face, pointed toward the dead garden and not toward me, sagged. There was a certain unnatural sparkle in his eyes that might have been tears.

"Aw, Dad, they're okay—"

"Of course they are. A thief and two feebs. Fine company for my son."

"Vern Tessio isn't feeble," I said. Teddy was a harder case to argue.

"Twelve years old and still in the fifth grade," my dad said. "And that time he slept over. When the Sunday paper came the next morning, he took an hour and a half to read the funny-pages."

That made me mad, because I didn't think he was being fair. He was judging Vern the way he judged all my friends, from having seen them off and on, mostly going in and out of the house. He was wrong about them. And when he called Chris a thief I always saw red, because he didn't know *any-thing* about Chris. I wanted to tell him that, but if I pissed him off he'd keep me home. And he wasn't really mad anyway, not like he got at the supper-table sometimes, ranting so loud that nobody wanted to eat. Now he just looked sad and tired and used. He was sixty-three years old, old enough to be my grandfather.

My mom was fifty-five—no spring chicken, either. When she and dad got married they tried to start a family right away and my mom got pregnant and had a miscarriage. She miscarried two more and the doctor told her she'd never be able to carry a baby to term. I got all of this stuff, chapter and verse, whenever one of them was lecturing me, you understand. They wanted me to think I was a special delivery from God and I wasn't appreciating my great good fortune in being conceived when my mother was forty-two and starting to gray. I wasn't appreciating my great good fortune and I wasn't appreciating her tremendous pain and sacrifices, either.

Five years after the doctor said Mom would never have a baby she got pregnant with Dennis. She carried him for eight months and then he just sort of fell out, all eight pounds of him—my father used to say that if she had carried Dennis to term, the kid would have weighed fifteen pounds. The doctor said: Well, sometimes nature fools us, but he'll be the only one you'll ever have. Thank God for him and be content. Ten years later she got pregnant with me. She not only carried me to term, the doctor had to use forceps to yank me out. Did you ever hear of such a fucked-up family? I came into the world the child of two Geritol-chuggers, not to go on and on about it, and my only brother was playing league baseball in the big kids' park before I even got out of diapers.

In the case of my mom and dad, one gift from God had been enough. I won't say they treated me badly, and they sure never beat me, but I was a hell of a big surprise and I guess when you get into your forties you're not as partial to surprises as you were in your twenties. After I was born, Mom got the operation her hen-party friends referred to as "The Band-Aid." I guess she wanted to make a hundred percent sure that there wouldn't be any more gifts from God. When I got to college I found out I'd beaten long odds just by not being born retarded . . . although I think my dad had his doubts when he saw my friend Vern taking ten minutes to puzzle out the dialogue in Beetle Baily.

This business about being ignored: I could never really pin it down until I did a book report in high school on this novel called *The Invisible Man*. When I agreed to do the book for Miss Hardy I thought it was going to be the science fiction story about the guy in bandages and Foster Grants—Claude Rains played him in the movies. When I found out this was a different story I tried to give the book back but Miss Hardy wouldn't let me off the hook. I ended up being real glad. This *Invisible Man* is about a Negro. Nobody ever notices him at all unless he fucks up. People look right through him. When he talks, nobody answers. He's like a black ghost. Once I got into it, I ate that book up like it was a John D. MacDonald, because that cat Ralph Ellison was writing about *me*. At the supper-table it was Denny how many did you strike out and Denny who asked you to the Sadie Hawkins dance and Denny I want to talk to you man to man about that car we were looking at. I'd say: "Pass the butter," and Dad would say: Denny, are you sure the Army is what you want? I'd say: "Pass the butter someone, okay?" and Mom would ask Denny if he wanted her to pick him up one of the Pendleton shirts on sale downtown, and I'd end up getting the butter myself. One night when I was nine, just to see what would happen: I said, "Please pass those goddam spuds." And my mom said: Denny, Auntie Grace called today and she asked after you and Gordon.

The night Dennis graduated with honors from Castle Rock

High School I played sick and stayed home. I got Stevie Dara-
bont's oldest brother Royce to buy me a bottle of Wild Irish
Rose and I drank half of it and puked in my bed in the middle
of the night.

In a family situation like that, you're supposed to either
hate the older brother or idolize him hopelessly—at least that's
what they teach you in college psychology. Bullshit, right? But
so far as I can tell, I didn't feel either way about Dennis. We
rarely argued and never had a fist-fight. That would have been
ridiculous. Can you see a fourteen-year-old boy finding something to beat up his four-year-old brother about? And our folks
were always a little too impressed with him to burden him
with the care of his kid brother, so he never resented me the
way some older kids come to resent their sibs. When Denny
took me with him somewhere, it was of his own free will, and
those were some of the happiest times I can remember.

"Hey Lachance, who the fuck is that?"

*"My kid brother and you better watch your mouth, Davis. He'll
beat the crap out of you. Gordie's tough."*

*They gather around me for a moment, huge, impossibly tall, just a
moment of interest like a patch of sun. They are so big, they are so old.*

"Hey kid! This wet end really your big brother?"

I nod shyly.

"He's a real asshole, ain't he, kid?"

*I nod again and everybody, Dennis included, roars with laughter.
Then Dennis claps his hands together twice, briskly, and says: "Come
on, we gonna have a practice or stand around here like a bunch of
pussies?"*

*They run to their positions, already peppering the ball around the
infield.*

*"Go sit over there on the bench, Gordie. Be quiet. Don't bother
anybody."*

I go sit over there on the bench. I am good. I feel impossibly small under the sweet summer clouds. I watch my brother pitch. I don't bother anybody.

But there weren't many times like that.

Sometimes he read me bedtime stories that were better than Mom's; Mom's stories were about The Gingerbread Man and The Three Little Pigs, okay stuff, but Dennis's were about stuff like Bluebeard and Jack the Ripper. He also had a version of Billy Goat's Gruff where the troll under the bridge ended up the winner. And, as I have already said, he taught me the game of cribbage and how to do a box-shuffle. Not that much, but hey! in this world you take what you can get, am I right?

As I grew older, my feelings of love for Dennis were replaced with an almost clinical awe, the kind of awe so-so Christians feel for God, I guess. And when he died, I was mildly shocked and mildly sad, the way I imagine those same so-so Christians must have felt when *Time* magazine said God was dead. Let me put it this way: I was as sad for Denny's dying as I was when I heard on the radio that Dan Blocker had died. I'd seen them both about as frequently, and Denny never even got any re-runs.

He was buried in a closed coffin with the American flag on top (they took the flag off the box before they finally stuck it in the ground and folded it—the flag, not the box—into a cocked hat and gave it to my mom). My parents just fell to pieces. Four months hadn't been long enough to put them back together again; I didn't know if they'd *ever* be whole again. Mr. and Mrs. Dumpty. Denny's room was in suspended animation just one door down from my room, suspended animation or maybe in a time-warp. The Ivy League college pennants were still on the walls, and the senior pictures of the girls he had dated were still tucked into the mirror where he had stood for what seemed like hours at a stretch, combing his hair back into a ducktail like Elvis's. The stack of *Trues* and *Sports Illustrated* remained on his desk, their dates looking

25

more and more antique as time passed. It's the kind of thing you see in sticky-sentimental movies. But it wasn't sentimental to me; it was terrible. I didn't go into Dennis's room unless I had to because I kept expecting that he would be behind the door, or under the bed, or in the closet. Mostly it was the closet that preyed on my mind, and if my mother sent me in to get Denny's postcard album or his shoebox of photographs so she could look at them, I would imagine that door swinging slowly open while I stood rooted to the spot with horror. I would imagine him pallid and bloody in the darkness, the side of his head walloped in, a gray-veined cake of blood and brains drying on his shirt. I would imagine his arms coming up, his bloody hands hooking into claws, and he would be croaking: *It should have been you, Gordon. It should have been you.*

7

Stud City, by Gordon Lachance. Originally published in *Greenspun Quarterly,* Issue 45, Fall, 1970. Used by permission.

March.

Chico stands at the window, arms crossed, elbows on the ledge that divides upper and lower panes, naked, looking out, breath fogging the glass. A draft against his belly. Bottom right pane is gone. Blocked by a piece of cardboard.

"Chico."

He doesn't turn. She doesn't speak again. He can see a ghost of her in the glass, in his bed, sitting, blankets pulled up in apparent defiance of gravity. Her eye makeup has smeared into deep hollows under her eyes.

Chico shifts his gaze beyond her ghost, out beyond the house. Raining. Patches of snow sloughed away to reveal the bald ground underneath. He sees last year's dead grass, a plastic toy—Billy's—a rusty

26

rake. His brother Johnny's Dodge is up on blocks, the detired wheels sticking out like stumps. He remembers times he and Johnny worked on it, listening to the super-hits and boss oldies from WLAM in Lewiston pour out of Johnny's old transistor radio—a couple of times Johnny would give him a beer. *She gonna run fast, Chico,* Johnny would say. *She gonna eat up everything on this road from Gates Falls to Castle Rock. Wait till we get that Hearst shifter in her!*

But that had been then, and this was now.

Beyond Johnny's Dodge was the highway. Route 14, goes to Portland and New Hampshire south, all the way to Canada north, if you turned left on U.S. 1 at Thomaston.

"Stud City," Chico says to the glass. He smokes his cigarette.

"What?"

"Nothing, babe."

"Chico?" Her voice is puzzled. He will have to change the sheets before Dad gets back. She bled.

"What?"

"I love you, Chico."

"That's right."

Dirty March. *You're some old whore,* Chico thinks. *Dirty, staggering old baggy-tits March with rain in her face.*

"This room used to be Johnny's," he says suddenly.

"Who?"

"My brother."

"Oh. Where is he?"

"In the Army," Chico says, but Johnny isn't in the Army. He had been working the summer before at Oxford Plains Speedway and a car went out of control and skidded across the infield toward the pit area, where Johnny had been changing the back tires on a Chevy Charger-class stocker. Some guys shouted at him to look out, but Johnny never heard them. One of the guys who shouted was Johnny's brother Chico.

"Aren't you cold?" she asks.

"No. Well, my feet. A little."

And he thinks suddenly: *Well, my God. Nothing happened to Johnny that isn't going to happen to you, too, sooner or later.* He sees it again, though: the skidding, skating Ford Mustang, the knobs of his brother's spine picked out in a series of dimpled shadows against the white of his Hanes tee-shirt; he had been hunkered down, pulling one of the Chevy's back tires. There had been time to see rubber flaying off the tires of the runaway Mustang, to see its hanging muffler scraping up sparks from the infield. It had struck Johnny even as Johnny tried to get to his feet. Then the yellow shout of flame.

Well, Chico thinks, *it could have been slow,* and he thinks of his grandfather. Hospital smells. Pretty young nurses bearing bedpans. A last papery breath. Were there any good ways?

He shivers and wonders about God. He touches the small silver St. Christopher's medal that hangs on a chain around his neck. He is not a Catholic and he's surely not a Mexican: his real name is Edward May and his friends all call him Chico because his hair is black and he greases it back with Brylcreem and he wears boots with pointed toes and Cuban heels. Not Catholic, but he wears this medallion. Maybe if Johnny had been wearing one, the runaway Mustang would have missed him. You never knew.

He smokes and stares out the window and behind him the girl gets out of bed and comes to him quickly, almost mincing, maybe afraid he will turn around and look at her. She puts a warm hand on his back. Her breasts push against his side. Her belly touches his buttock.

"Oh. It *is* cold."

"It's this place."

"Do you love me, Chico?"

"You bet!" he says off-handedly, and then, more seriously: "You were cherry."

"What does that—"

"You were a virgin."

The hand reaches higher. One finger traces the skin on the nape of his neck. "I said, didn't I?"

"Was it hard? Did it hurt?"

She laughs. "No. But I was scared."

They watch the rain. A new Oldsmobile goes by on 14, spraying up water.

"Stud City," Chico says.

"What?"

"That guy. He's going Stud City. In his new stud car."

She kisses the place her finger has been touching gently and he brushes at her as if she were a fly.

"What's the matter?"

He turns to her. Her eyes flick down to his penis and then up again hastily. Her arms twitch to cover herself, and then she remembers that they never do stuff like that in the movies and she drops them to her sides again. Her hair is black and her skin is winter white, the color of cream. Her breasts are firm, her belly perhaps a little too soft. One flaw to remind, Chico thinks, that this isn't the movies.

"Jane?"

"What?" He can feel himself getting ready. Not beginning, but getting ready.

"It's all right," he says. "We're friends." He eyes her deliberately, letting himself reach at her in all sorts of ways. When he looks at her face again, it is flushed. "Do you mind me looking at you?"

"I . . . no. No, Chico."

She steps back, closes her eyes, sits on the bed, and leans back, legs spread. He sees all of her. The muscles, the little muscles on the insides of her thighs . . . they're jumping, uncontrolled, and this suddenly excites him more than the taut cones of her breasts or the mild pink pearl of her cunt. Excitement trembles in him, some stupid Bozo on a spring. Love may be as divine as the poets say, he thinks, but sex is Bozo the Clown bouncing around on a spring. How could a woman look at an erect penis without going off into mad gales of laughter?

The rain beats against the roof, against the window, against the sodden cardboard patch blocking the glass-less lower pane. He presses his hand against his chest, looking for a moment like a stage Roman about to orate. His hand is cold. He drops it to his side.

"Open your eyes. We're friends, I said."

Obediently, she opens them. She looks at him. Her eyes appear violet now. The rainwater running down the window makes rippling patterns on her face, her neck, her breasts. Stretched across the bed, her belly has been pulled tight. She is perfect in her moment.

"Oh," she says. "Oh Chico, it feels so *funny.*" A shiver goes through her. She has curled her toes involuntarily. He can see the insteps of her feet. Her insteps are pink. "Chico. Chico."

He steps toward her. His body is shivering and her eyes widen. She says something, one word, but he can't tell what it is. This isn't the time to ask. He half-kneels before her for just a second, looking at the floor with frowning concentration, touching her legs just above the knees. He measures the tide within himself. Its pull is thoughtless, fantastic. He pauses a little longer.

The only sound is the tinny tick of the alarm clock on the bedtable, standing brassy-legged atop a pile of Spiderman comic books. Her breathing flutters faster and faster. His muscles slide smoothly as he dives upward and forward. They begin. It's better this time. Outside, the rain goes on washing away the snow.

A half-hour later Chico shakes her out of a light doze. "We gotta move," he says. "Dad and Virginia will be home pretty quick."

She looks at her wristwatch and sits up. This time she makes no attempt to shield herself. Her whole tone—her body English—has changed. She has not matured (although she probably believes she has) or learned anything more complex than tying a shoe, but her tone has changed just the same. He nods and she smiles tentatively at him. He reaches for the cigarettes on the bedtable. As she draws on her panties, he thinks of a line from an old novelty song: *Keep playin till I shoot through, Blue . . . play your digeree, do.* "Tie Me Kangaroo Down," by Rolf Harris. He grins. That was a song Johnny used to sing. It ended: *So we tanned his hide when he died, Clyde, and that's it hanging on the shed.*

30

She hooks her bra and begins buttoning her blouse. "What are you smiling about, Chico?"

"Nothing," he says.

"Zip me up?"

He goes to her, still naked, and zips her up. He kisses her cheek. "Go on in the bathroom and do your face if you want," he says. "Just don't take too long, okay?"

She goes up the hall gracefully, and Chico watches her, smoking. She is a tall girl—taller than he—and she has to duck her head a little going through the bathroom door. Chico finds his underpants under the bed. He puts them in the dirty clothes bag hanging just inside the closet door, and gets another pair from the bureau. He puts them on, and then, while walking back to the bed, he slips and almost falls in a patch of wetness the square of cardboard has let in.

"Goddam," he whispers resentfully.

He looks around at the room, which had been Johnny's until Johnny died *(why did I tell her he was in the* Army, *for Christ's sake? he* wonders . . . a little uneasily). Fiberboard walls, so thin he can hear Dad and Virginia going at it at night, that don't quite make it all the way to the ceiling. The floor has a slightly crazy hipshot angle so that the room's door will only stay open if you block it open—if you forget, it swings stealthily closed as soon as your back is turned. On the far wall is a movie poster from *Easy Rider—Two Men Went Looking for America and Couldn't Find It Anywhere.* The room had more life when Johnny lived here. Chico doesn't know how or why; only that it's true. And he knows something else, as well. He knows that sometimes the room spooks him at night. Sometimes he thinks that the closet door will swing open and Johnny will be standing there, his body charred and twisted and blackened, his teeth yellow dentures poking out of wax that has partially melted and re-hardened; and Johnny will be whispering: *Get out of my room, Chico. And if you lay a hand on my Dodge, I'll fuckin kill you. Got it?*

Got it, bro, Chico thinks.

For a moment he stands still, looking at the rumpled sheet spotted with

31

the girl's blood, and then he spreads the blankets up in one quick gesture. Here. Right here. How do you like that, Virginia? How does that grab your snatch? He puts on his pants, his engineer boots, finds a sweater.

He's dry-combing his hair in front of the mirror when she comes out of the john. She looks classy. Her too-soft stomach doesn't show in the jumper. She looks at the bed, does a couple of things to it, and it comes out looking made instead of just spread up.

"Good," Chico says.

She laughs a little self-consciously and pushes a lock of hair behind her ear. It is an evocative, poignant gesture.

"Let's go," he says.

They go out through the hall and the living room. Jane pauses in front of the tinted studio photograph on top of the TV. It shows his father and Virginia, a high-school-age Johnny, a grammar-school-age Chico, and an infant Billy—in the picture, Johnny is holding Billy. All of them have fixed, stone grins . . . all except Virginia, whose face is its sleepy, indecipherable self. That picture, Chico remembers, was taken less than a month after his dad married the bitch.

"That your mother and father?"

"It's my father," Chico says. "She's my stepmother, Virginia. Come on."

"Is she still that pretty?" Jane asks, picking up her coat and handing Chico his windbreaker.

"I guess my old man thinks so," Chico says.

They step out into the shed. It's a damp and drafty place—the wind hoots through the cracks in its slapstick walls. There is a pile of old bald tires, Johnny's old bike that Chico inherited when he was ten and which he promptly wrecked, a pile of detective magazines, returnable Pepsi bottles, a greasy monolithic engine block, an orange crate full of paperback books, an old paint-by-numbers of a horse standing on dusty green grass.

Chico helps her pick her way outside. The rain is falling with disheartening steadiness. Chico's old sedan stands in a driveway puddle, looking downhearted. Even up on blocks and with a piece of plastic covering the place where the windshield should go, Johnny's Dodge has more class. Chico's car is a Buick. The paint is dull and flowered with spots of rust. The front seat upholstery has been covered with a brown Army blanket. A large button pinned to the sun visor on the passenger side says: I WANT IT EVERY DAY. There is a rusty starter assembly on the back seat; if it ever stops raining he will clean it, he thinks, and maybe put it into the Dodge. Or maybe not.

The Buick smells musty and his own starter grinds a long time before the Buick starts up.

"Is it your battery?" she asks.

"Just the goddam rain, I guess." He backs out onto the road, flicking on the windshield wipers and pausing for a moment to look at the house. It is a completely unappetizing aqua color. The shed sticks off from it at a ragtag, double-jointed angle, tarpaper and peeled-looking shingles.

The radio comes on with a blare and Chico shuts it off at once. There is the beginning of a Sunday afternoon headache behind his forehead. They ride past the Grange hall and the Volunteer Fire Department and Brownie's Store. Sally Morrison's T-Bird is parked by Brownie's hi-test pump, and Chico raises a hand to her as he turns off onto the old Lewiston road.

"Who's that?"

"Sally Morrison."

"Pretty lady." Very neutral.

He feels for his cigarettes. "She's been married twice and divorced twice. Now she's the town pump, if you believe half the talk that goes on in this shitass little town."

"She looks young."

"She is."

"Have you ever—"

He slides his hand up her leg and smiles. "No," he says. "My brother, maybe, but not me. I like Sally, though. She's got her alimony and her big white Bird, she doesn't care what people say about her."

It starts to seem like a long drive. The Androscoggin, off to the right, is slaty and sullen. The ice is all out of it now. Jane has grown quiet and thoughtful. The only sound is the steady snap of the windshield wipers. When the car rolls through the dips in the road there is groundfog, waiting for evening when it will creep out of these pockets and take over the whole River Road.

They cross into Auburn and Chico drives the cutoff and swings onto Minot Avenue. The four lanes are nearly deserted, and all the suburban homes look packaged. They see one little boy in a yellow plastic raincoat walking up the sidewalk, carefully stepping in all the puddles.

"Go, man," Chico says softly.

"What?" Jane asks.

"Nothing, babe. Go back to sleep."

She laughs a little doubtfully.

Chico turns up Keston Street and into the driveway of one of the packaged houses. He doesn't turn off the ignition.

"Come in and I'll give you cookies," she says.

He shakes his head. "I have to get back."

"I know." She puts her arms around him and kisses him. "Thank you for the most wonderful time of my life."

He smiles suddenly. His face shines. It is nearly magical. "I'll see you Monday, Janey-Jane. Still friends, right?"

"You know we are," she says, and kisses him again . . . but when he cups a breast through her jumper, she pulls away. "Don't. My father might see."

He lets her go, only a little of the smile left. She gets out of the car quickly and runs through the rain to the back door. A second later she's gone. Chico pauses for a moment to light a cigarette and then he backs out of the driveway. The Buick stalls and the starter seems to grind forever before the engine manages to catch. It is a long ride home.

When he gets there, Dad's station wagon is parked in the driveway. He pulls in beside it and lets the engine die. For a moment he sits inside silently, listening to the rain. It is like being inside a steel drum.

Inside, Billy is watching Carl Stormer and His Country Buckaroos on the TV set. When Chico comes in, Billy jumps up, excited. "Eddie, hey Eddie, you know what Uncle Pete said? He said him and a whole mess of other guys sank a kraut sub in the war! Will you take me to the show next Saturday?"

"I don't know," Chico says, grinning. "Maybe if you kiss my shoes every night before supper all week." He pulls Billy's hair. Billy hollers and laughs and kicks him in the shins.

"Cut it out, now," Sam May says, coming into the room. "Cut it out, you two. You know how your mother feels about the rough-housing." He has pulled his tie down and unbuttoned the top button of his shirt. He's got a couple-three red hotdogs on a plate. The hotdogs are wrapped in white bread, and Sam May has put the old mustard right to them. "Where you been, Eddie?"

"At Jane's."

The toilet flushes in the bathroom. Virginia. Chico wonders briefly if Jane has left any hairs in the sink, or a lipstick, or a bobby pin.

"You should have come with us to see your Uncle Pete and Aunt Ann," his father says. He eats a frank in three quick bites. "You're getting to be like a stranger around here, Eddie. I don't like that. Not while we provide the bed and board."

"Some bed," Chico says. "Some board."

Sam looks up quickly, hurt at first, then angry. When he speaks, Chico sees that his teeth are yellow with French's mustard. He feels vaguely nauseated. "Your lip. Your goddam lip. You aren't too big yet, snotnose."

Chico shrugs, peels a slice of Wonder Bread off the loaf standing on the TV tray by his father's chair, and spreads it with ketchup. "In three months I'm going to be gone anyway."

"What the hell are you talking about?"

"I'm gonna fix up Johnny's car and go out to California. Look for work."

"Oh, yeah. Right." He is a big man, big in a shambling way, but Chico thinks now that he got smaller after he married Virginia, and smaller again after Johnny died. And in his mind he hears himself saying to Jane: *My brother, maybe, but not me.* And on the heels of that: *Play your dig-*

35

eree, do, Blue. "You ain't never going to get that car as far as Castle Rock, let alone California."

"You don't think so? Just watch my fucking dust."

For a moment his father only looks at him and then he throws the frank he has been holding. It hits Chico in the chest, spraying mustard on his sweater and on the chair.

"Say that word again and I'll break your nose for you, smartass."

Chico picks up the frank and looks at it. Cheap red frank, smeared with French's mustard. Spread a little sunshine. He throws it back at his father. Sam gets up, his face the color of an old brick, the vein in the middle of his forehead pulsing. His thigh connects with the TV tray and it overturns. Billy stands in the kitchen doorway watching them. He's gotten himself a plate of franks and beans and the plate has tipped and beanjuice runs onto the floor. Billy's eyes are wide, his mouth trembling. On the TV, Carl Stormer and His Country Buckaroos are tearing through "Long Black Veil" at a breakneck pace.

"You raise them up best you can and they spit on you," his father says thickly. "Ayuh. That's how it goes." He gropes blindly on the seat of his chair and comes up with the half-eaten hotdog. He holds it in his fist like a severed phallus. Incredibly, he begins to eat it . . . at the same time, Chico sees that he has begun to cry. "Ayuh, they spit on you, that's just how it goes."

"Well, why in the hell did you have to marry *her*?" he bursts out, and then has to bite down on the rest of it: *If you hadn't married her, Johnny would still be alive.*

"That's none of your goddam business!" Sam May roars through his tears. "That's my business!"

"Oh?" Chico shouts back. "Is that so? I only have to live with her! Me and Billy, we have to live with her! Watch her grind you down! And you don't even know—"

"What?" his father says, and his voice is suddenly low and ominous. The chunk of hotdog left in his closed fist is like a bloody chunk of bone. "What don't I know?"

"You don't know shit from Shinola," he says, appalled at what has almost come out of his mouth.

"You want to stop it now," his father says. "Or I'll beat the hell out of you, Chico." He only calls him this when he is very angry indeed.

Chico turns and sees that Virginia is standing at the other side of the room, adjusting her skirt minutely, looking at him with her large, calm, brown eyes. Her eyes are beautiful; the rest of her is not so beautiful, so self-renewing, but those eyes will carry her for years yet, Chico thinks, and he feels the sick hate come back—*So we tanned his hide when he died, Clyde, and that's it hanging on the shed.*

"She's got you pussywhipped and you don't have the guts to do anything about it!"

All of this shouting has finally become too much for Billy—he gives a great wail of terror, drops his plate of franks and beans, and covers his face with his hands. Beanjuice splatters his Sunday shoes and sprays across the rug.

Sam takes a single step forward and then stops when Chico makes a curt beckoning gesture, as if to say: *Yeah, come on, let's get down to it, what took you so fuckin long?* They stand like statues until Virginia speaks—her voice is low, as calm as her brown eyes.

"Have you had a girl in your room, Ed? You know how your father and I feel about that." Almost as an afterthought: "She left a handkerchief."

He stares at her, savagely unable to express the way he feels, the way she is dirty, the way she shoots unerringly at the back, the way she clips in behind you and cuts your hamstrings.

You could hurt me if you wanted to, the calm brown eyes say. *I know you know what was going on before he died. But that's the only way you can hurt me, isn't it, Chico? And only then if your father believed you. And if he believed you, it would kill him.*

His father lunges at the new gambit like a bear. "Have you been screwing in my house, you little bastard?"

"Watch your language, please, Sam," Virginia says calmly.

"Is that why you didn't want to come with us? So you could scr—so you could—"

"*Say it!*" Chico weeps. "Don't let her do it to you! Say it! Say what you mean!"

"Get out," he says dully. "Don't you come back until you can apologize to your mother and me."

"Don't you dare!" he cries. "Don't you dare call that bitch my mother! I'll kill you!"

"Stop it, Eddie!" Billy screams. The words are muffled, blurred through his hands, which still cover his face. "Stop yelling at Daddy! Stop it, *please!*"

Virginia doesn't move from the doorway. Her calm eyes remain on Chico.

Sam blunders back a step and the backs of his knees strike the edge of his easy chair. He sits down in it heavily and averts his face against a hairy forearm. "I can't even look at you when you got words like that in your mouth, Eddie. You are making me feel so bad."

"*She* makes you feel bad! Why don't you admit it?"

He does not reply. Still not looking at Chico, he fumbles another frank wrapped in bread from the plate on the TV tray. He fumbles for the mustard. Billy goes on crying. Carl Stormer and His Country Buckaroos are singing a truck-driving song. "My rig is old, but that don't mean she's slow," Carl tells all his western Maine viewers.

"The boy doesn't know what he's saying, Sam," Virginia says gently. "It's hard, at his age. It's hard to grow up."

She's whipped him. That's the end, all right.

He turns and heads for the door which leads first into the shed and then outdoors. As he opens it he looks back at Virginia, and she gazes at him tranquilly when he speaks her name.

"What is it, Ed?"

"The sheets are bloody." He pauses. "I broke her in."

He thinks something has stirred in her eyes, but that is probably only his wish. "Please go now, Ed. You're scaring Billy."

He leaves. The Buick doesn't want to start and he has almost resigned himself to walking in the rain when the engine finally catches. He lights a cigarette and backs out onto 14, slamming the clutch back in and racing the mill when it starts to jerk and splutter. The generator light blinks balefully at him twice, and then the car settles into a ragged idle. At last he is on his way, creeping up the road toward Gates Falls.

He spares Johnny's Dodge one last look.

Johnny could have had steady work at Gates Mills & Weaving, but only on the night shift. Nightwork didn't bother him, he had told Chico, and the pay was better than at the Plains, but their father worked days, and working nights at the mill would have meant Johnny would have been home with her, home alone or with Chico in the next room . . . and the walls were thin. *I can't stop and she won't let me try,* Johnny said. *Yeah, I know what it would do to him. But she's . . . she just won't stop and it's like I* can't *stop . . . she's always at me, you know what I mean, you've seen her, Billy's too young to understand, but you've seen her . . .*

Yes. He had seen her. And Johnny had gone to work at the Plains, telling their father it was because he could get parts for the Dodge on the cheap. And that's how it happened that he had been changing a tire when the Mustang came skidding and skating across the infield with its muffler draggin up sparks; that was how his stepmother had killed his brother, so just keep playing until I shoot through, Blue, cause we goin Stud City right here in this shitheap Buick, and he remembers how the rubber smelled, and how the knobs of Johnny's spine cast small crescent shadows on the bright white of his tee-shirt, he remembers seeing Johnny get halfway up from the squat he had been working in when the Mustang hit him, squashing him between it and the Chevy, and there had been a hollow bang as the Chevy came down off its jacks, and then the bright yellow flare of flame, the rich smell of gasoline—

Chico strikes the brakes with both feet, bringing the sedan to a crunching, juddering halt on the sodden shoulder. He leans wildly across the seat, throws open the passenger door, and sprays yellow puke onto the mud and snow. The sight of it makes him puke again, and the thought of it makes him dry-heave one more time. The car almost stalls, but he catches it in time. The generator light winks out reluctantly when he guns the engine. He sits, letting the shakes work their way out of him. A car goes by him fast, a new Ford, white, throwing up great dirty fans of water and slush.

"Stud City," Chico says. "In his new stud car. Funky."

He tastes puke on his lips and in his throat and coating his sinuses. He doesn't want a cigarette. Danny Carter will let him sleep over. Tomorrow will be time enough for further decisions. He pulls back onto Route 14 and gets rolling.

8

Pretty fucking melodramatic, right?

The world has seen one or two better stories, I know that—one or two hundred thousand better ones, more like it. It ought to have THIS IS A PRODUCT OF AN UNDERGRADUATE CREATIVE WRITING WORKSHOP stamped on every page . . . because that's just what it was, at least up to a certain point. It seems both painfully derivative and painfully sophomoric to me now; style by Hemingway (except we've got the whole thing in the present tense for some reason—how too fucking trendy), theme by Faulkner. Could anything be more *serious?* More *lit'ry?*

But even its pretensions can't hide the fact that it's an extremely sexual story written by an extremely inexperienced young man (at the time I wrote "Stud City," I had been to bed with two girls and had ejaculated prematurely all over one of them—not much like Chico in the foregoing tale, I guess). Its attitude toward women goes beyond hostility and to a point which verges on actual ugliness—two of the women in "Stud City" are sluts, and the third is a simple receptacle who says things like "I love you, Chico" and "Come in, I'll give you cookies." Chico, on the other hand, is a macho cigarette-smoking working-class hero who could have stepped whole and breathing from the grooves of a Bruce Springsteen record—although Springsteen was yet to be heard from when I published the story in the college literary magazine (where it ran between a poem called "Images of Me" and an essay on student parietals written entirely in lower case). It is the work of a young man every bit as insecure as he was inexperienced.

And yet it was the first story I ever wrote that felt like *my* story—the first one that really felt *whole,* after five years of trying. The first one that might still be able to stand up, even with its props taken away. Ugly but alive. Even now when I read it, stifling a smile at its pseudo-toughness and its pretensions, I can see the true face of Gordon Lachance lurking just behind the lines of print, a Gordon Lachance younger than the one living and writing now, one certainly more idealistic than the best-selling novelist who is more apt to have his paperback contracts reviewed than his books, but not so young as the one who went with his friends that day to see the body of a dead kid named Ray Brower. A Gordon Lachance halfway along in the process of losing the shine.

No, it's not a very good story—its author was too busy listening to other voices to listen as closely as he should have to the one coming from inside. But it was the first time I had ever really used the place I knew and the things I felt in a piece of fiction, and there was a kind of dreadful exhilaration in seeing things that had troubled me for years come out in a new form, *a form over which I had imposed control.* It had been years since that childhood idea of Denny being in the closet of his spookily preserved room had occurred to me; I would have honestly believed I had forgotten it. Yet there it is in "Stud City," only slightly changed . . . but *controlled.*

I've resisted the urge to change it a lot more, to rewrite it, to juice it up—and that urge was fairly strong, because I find the story quite embarrassing now. But there are still things in it I like, things that would be cheapened by changes made by this later Lachance, who has the first threads of gray in his hair. Things, like that image of the shadows on Johnny's white tee-shirt or that of the rain-ripples on Jane's naked body, that seem better than they have any right to be.

Also, it was the first story I never showed to my mother and father. There was too much Denny in it. Too much Castle Rock. And most of all, too much 1960. You always know the truth, because when you cut yourself or someone else with it, there's always a bloody show.

9

My room was on the second floor, and it must have been at least ninety degrees up there. It would be a hundred and ten by after-noon, even with all the windows open. I was really glad I wasn't sleeping there that night, and the thought of where we were going made me excited all over again. I made two blankets into a bedroll and tied it with my old belt. I collected all my money, which was sixty-eight cents. Then I was ready to go.

I went down the back stairs to avoid meeting my dad in front of the house, but I hadn't needed to worry; he was still out in the garden with the hose, making useless rainbows in the air and looking through them.

I walked down Summer Street and cut through a vacant lot to Carbine—where the offices of the Castle Rock *Call* stand today. I was headed up Carbine toward the clubhouse when a car pulled over to the curb and Chris got out. He had his old Boy Scout pack in one hand and two blankets rolled up and tied with clothesrope in the other.

"Thanks, mister," he said, and trotted over to join me as the car pulled away. His Boy Scout canteen was slung around his neck and under one arm so that it finally ended up banging on his hip. His eyes were sparkling.

"Gordie! You wanna see something?"

"Sure, I guess so. What?"

"Come on down here first." He pointed at the narrow space between the Blue Point Diner and the Castle Rock Drugstore.

"What is it, Chris?"

"Come on, I said!"

He ran down the alley and after a brief moment (that's all it took me to cast aside my better judgment) I ran after him. The two buildings were set slightly toward each other rather than running parallel, and so the alley narrowed as it went back. We waded through trashy drifts of old newspapers and stepped over cruel, sparkly nests of broken beer and soda bottles. Chris cut behind the Blue Point and put his bedroll down. There were eight or nine garbage cans lined up here and the stench was incredible.

"Phew! Chris! Come on, gimme a break!"

"Gimme your arm," Chris said, by rote.

"No, sincerely, I'm gonna throw u—"

The words broke off in my mouth and I forgot all about the smelly garbage cans. Chris had unslung his pack and opened it and reached inside. Now he was holding out a huge pistol with dark wood grips.

"You wanna be the Lone Ranger or the Cisco Kid?" Chris asked, grinning.

"Walking, talking Jesus! Where'd you get that?"

"Hawked it out of my dad's bureau. It's a forty-five."

"Yeah, I can see that," I said, although it could have been a .38 or a .357 for all I knew—in spite of all the John D. Mac-Donalds and Ed McBains I'd read, the only pistol I'd ever seen up close was the one Constable Bannerman carried . . . and although all the kids asked him to take it out of its holster, Bannerman never would. "Man, your dad's gonna hide you when he finds out. You said he was on a mean streak *anyway*."

His eyes just went on dancing. "That's *it,* man. He ain't gonna find out *nothing.* Him and these other rummies are all laid up down in Harrison with six or eight bottles of wine. They won't be back for a week. Fucking rummies." His lip curled. He was the only guy in our gang who would never take a drink, even to show he had, you know, big balls. He said he wasn't going to grow up to be a fucking tosspot like his old man. And he told me once privately—this was after the DeSpain twins showed up with a six-pack they'd hawked from their old man and everybody teased Chris because he wouldn't take a beer or even a swallow—that he was *scared* to drink. He said his father never got his nose all the way out of the bottle anymore, that his older brother had been drunk out of his tits when he raped that girl, and that Eyeball was always guzzling Purple Jesuses with Ace Merrill and Charlie Hogan and Billy Tessio. What, he asked me, did I think his chances of letting go of the bottle would be once he picked it up? Maybe you think that's funny, a twelve-year-old worrying that he might be an incipient alcoholic, but it wasn't funny to Chris. Not at all. He'd thought about the possibility a lot. He'd had occasion to.

"You got shells for it?"

"Nine of them—all that was left in the box. He'll think he used em himself, shooting at cans while he was drunk."

"Is it loaded?"

"*No!* Chrissake, what do you think I *am?*"

I finally took the gun. I liked the heavy way it sat there in my hand. I could see myself as Steve Carella of the 87th Squad, going after that guy The Heckler or maybe covering Meyer Meyer or Kling while they broke into a desperate junkie's sleazy apartment. I sighted on one of the smelly trashcans and squeezed the trigger.

KA-BLAM!

The gun bucked in my hand. Fire licked from the end. It felt as if my wrist had just been broken. My heart vaulted nimbly into the back of my mouth and crouched there, trembling. A big hole appeared in the corrugated metal surface of the trashcan—it was the work of an evil conjuror.

"Jesus!" I screamed.

Chris was cackling wildly—in real amusement or hysterical terror I couldn't tell. "You did it, you did it! *Gordie did it!*" he bugled. *"Hey, Gordon Lachance is shooting up Castle Rock!"*

"Shut up! Let's get out of here!" I screamed, and grabbed him by the shirt.

As we ran, the back door of the Blue Point jerked open and Francine Tupper stepped out in her white rayon waitress's uniform. "Who did that? Who's letting off cherry-bombs back here?"

We ran like hell, cutting behind the drugstore and the hardware store and the Emporium Galorium, which sold antiques and junk and dime books. We climbed a fence, spiking our palms with splinters, and finally came out on Curran Street. I threw the .45 at Chris as we ran; he was killing himself laughing but caught it and somehow managed to stuff it back into his knapsack and close one of the snaps. Once around the corner of Curran and back on Carbine Street, we slowed to a walk so we wouldn't look suspicious, running in the heat. Chris was still giggling.

"Man, you shoulda seen your face. Oh man, that was priceless. That was really fine. My fucking-A." He shook his head and slapped his leg and howled.

"You knew it was loaded, didn't you? You wet! I'm gonna be in trouble. That Tupper babe saw me."

"Shit, she thought it was a firecracker. Besides, ole Thunder-jugs Tupper can't see past the end of her own nose, you know that. Thinks wearing glasses would spoil her *pret-ty face.*" He put one palm against the small of his back and bumped his hips and got laughing again.

"Well, I don't care. That was a mean trick, Chris. Really."

"Come on, Gordie." He put a hand on my shoulder. "I didn't know it was loaded, honest to God, I swear on my mother's name I just took it out of my dad's bureau. He always unloads it. He must have been really drunk when he put it away the last time."

"You really didn't load it?"

"No sir."

"You swear it on your mother's name even if she goes to hell for you telling a lie?"

"I swear." He crossed himself and spit, his face as open and repentant as any choirboy's. But when we turned into the vacant lot where our treehouse was and saw Vern and Teddy sitting on their bedrolls waiting for us, he started to laugh again. He told them the whole story, and after everybody had had their yucks, Teddy asked him what Chris thought they needed a pistol for.

"Nothin," Chris said. "Except we might see a bear. Something like that. Besides, it's spooky sleeping out at night in the woods."

Everybody nodded at that. Chris was the biggest, toughest guy in our gang, and he could always get away with saying things like that. Teddy, on the other hand, would have gotten his ass ragged off if he even hinted he was afraid of the dark.

"Did you set your tent up in the field?" Teddy asked Vern.

"Yeah. And I put two turned-on flashlights in it so it'll look like we're there after dark."

"Hot shit!" I said, and clapped Vern on the back. For him, that was thinking. He grinned and blushed.

"So let's go," Teddy said. "Come on, it's almost twelve already!"

Chris got up and we gathered around him.

"We'll walk across Beeman's field and behind that furniture place by Sonny's Texaco," he said. "Then we'll get on the railroad tracks down by the dump and just walk across the trestle into Harlow."

"How far do you think it's gonna be?" Teddy asked.

Chris shrugged. "Harlow's big. We're gonna be walking at least twenty miles. That sound right to you, Gordie?"

"Yeah. It might even be thirty."

"Even if it's thirty we ought to be there by tomorrow afternoon, if no one goes pussy."

"No pussies here," Teddy said at once.

We all looked at each other for a second.

"*Miaoww,*" Vern said, and we all laughed.

"Come on, you guys," Chris said, and shouldered his pack.

We walked out of the vacant lot together, Chris slightly in the lead.

10

By the time we got across Beeman's field and had struggled up the cindery embankment to the Great Southern and Western Maine tracks, we had all taken our shirts off and tied them around our waists. We were sweating like pigs. At the top of the embankment we looked down the tracks, toward where we'd have to go.

I'll never forget that moment, no matter how old I get. I was the only one with a watch—a cheap Timex I'd gotten as a premium for selling Cloverine Brand Salve the year before.

Its hands stood at straight up noon, and the sun beat down on the dry, shadeless vista before us with savage heat. You could feel it working to get in under your skull and fry your brains.

Behind us was Castle Rock, spread out on the long hill that was known as Castle View, surrounding its green and shady common. Further down Castle River you could see the stacks of the woollen mill spewing smoke into a sky the color of gunmetal and spewing waste into the water. The Jolly Furniture Barn was on our left. And straight ahead of us the railroad tracks, bright and heliographing in the sun. They paralleled the Castle River, which was on our left. To our right was a lot of overgrown scrubland (there's motorcycle track there today—they have scrambles every Sunday afternoon at 2:00 p.m.). An old abandoned water tower stood on the horizon, rusty and somehow scary.

We stood there for that one noontime moment and then Chris said impatiently, "Come on, let's get going."

We walked beside the tracks in the cinders, kicking up little puffs of blackish dust at every step. Our socks and sneakers were soon gritty with it. Vern started singing "Roll Me Over in the Clover" but soon quit it, which was a break for our ears. Only Teddy and Chris had brought canteens, and we were all hitting them pretty hard.

"We could fill the canteens again at the dump faucet," I said. "My dad told me that's a safe well. It's a hundred and ninety feet deep."

"Okay," Chris said, being the tough platoon leader. "That'll be a good place to take five, anyway."

"What about food?" Teddy asked suddenly. "I bet nobody thought to bring something to eat. I know I didn't."

Chris stopped. "Shit! I didn't, either. Gordie?"

I shook my head, wondering how I could have been so dumb.

"Vern?"

"Zip," Vern said. "Sorry."

"Well, let's see how much money we got," I said. I untied my shirt, spread it on the cinders, and dropped my own sixty-eight cents onto it. The coins glittered feverishly in the sunlight. Chris had a tattered dollar and two pennies. Teddy had two quarters and two nickels. Vern had exactly seven cents.

"Two-thirty-seven," I said. "Not bad. There's a store at the end of that little road that goes to the dump. Somebody'll have to walk down there and get some hamburger and some tonics while the others rest."

"Who?" Vern asked.

"We'll match for it when we get to the dump. Come on."

I slid all the money into my pants pocket and was just tying my shirt around my waist again when Chris hollered: *"Train!"*

I put my hand out on one of the rails to feel it, even though I could already hear it. The rail was thrumming crazily; for a moment it was like holding the train in my hand.

"Paratroops over the side!" Vern bawled, and leaped halfway down the embankment in one crazy, clownish stride. Vern was nuts for playing paratroops anyplace the ground was soft—a gravel pit, a haymow, an embankment like this one. Chris jumped after him. The train was really loud now, probably headed straight up our side of the river toward Lewiston. Instead of jumping, Teddy turned in the direction from which it was coming. His thick glasses glittered in the sun. His long hair flopped untidily over his brow in sweat-soaked stringers.

"Go on, Teddy," I said.

"No, huh-uh, I'm gonna dodge it." He looked at me, his magnified eyes frantic with excitement. "A train-dodge, dig it? What's trucks after a fuckin train-dodge?"

"You're crazy, man. You want to get killed?"

"Just like the beach at Normandy!" Teddy yelled, and strode out into the middle of the tracks. He stood on one of the cross-ties, lightly balanced.

I stood stunned for a moment, unable to believe stupidity of such width and breadth. Then I grabbed him, dragged him fighting and protesting to the embankment, and pushed him over. I jumped after him and Teddy caught me a good one in the guts while I was still in the air. The wind whooshed out of me, but I was still able to hit him in the sternum with my knee and knock him flat on his back before he could get all the way up. I landed, gasping and sprawling, and Teddy grabbed me around the neck. We went rolling all the way to the bottom of the embankment, hitting and clawing at each other while Chris and Vern stared at us, stupidly surprised.

"You little son of a bitch!" Teddy was screaming at me. "You fucker! Don't you throw your weight around on me! I'll kill you, you dipshit!"

I was getting my breath back now, and I made it to my feet. I backed away as Teddy advanced, holding my open hands up to slap away his punches, half-laughing and half-scared. Teddy was no one to fool around with when he went into one of his screaming fits. He'd take on a big kid in that state, and after the big kid broke both of his arms, he'd bite.

"Teddy, you can dodge anything you want after we see what we're going to see but

whack on the shoulder as one wildly swinging fist got past me

"until then no one's supposed to *see us,* you

whack on the side of the face, and then we might have had a real fight if Chris and Vern

"stupid wet end!"

hadn't grabbed us and kept us apart. Above us, the train roared by in a thunder of diesel exhaust and the great heavy clacking of boxcar wheels. A few cinders bounced down the embankment and the argument was over . . . at least until we could hear ourselves talk again.

It was only a short freight, and when the caboose had trailed by, Teddy said: "I'm gonna kill him. At least give him a fat lip." He struggled against Chris, but Chris only grabbed him tighter.

"Calm down, Teddy," Chris said quietly, and he kept saying it until Teddy stopped struggling and just stood there, his glasses hanging askew and his hearing-aid cord dangling limply against his chest on its way down to the battery, which he had shoved into the pocket of his jeans.

When he was completely still, Chris turned to me and said: "What the hell are you fighting with him about, Gordon?"

"He wanted to dodge the train. I figured the engineer would see him and report it. They might send a cop out."

"Ahhh, he'd be too busy makin chocolate in his drawers," Teddy said, but he didn't seem angry anymore. The storm had passed.

"Gordie was just trying to do the right thing," Vern said. "Come on, peace."

"Peace, you guys," Chris agreed.

"Yeah, okay," I said, and held out my hand, palm up. "Peace, Teddy?"

"I coulda dodged it," he said to me. "You know that, Gordie?"

"Yeah," I said, although the thought turned me cold inside. "I know it."

"Okay. Peace, then."

"Skin it, man," Chris ordered, and let go of Teddy.

Teddy slapped his hand down on mine hard enough to sting and then turned it over. I slapped his.

"Fuckin pussy Lachance," Teddy said.

"*Meeiowww,*" I said.

"Come on, you guys," Vern said. "Let's go, okay?"

51

"Go anywhere you want, but don't go here," Chris said solemnly, and Vern drew back as if to hit him.

11

We got to the dump around one-thirty, and Vern led the way down the embankment with a *Paratroops over the side!* We went to the bottom in big jumps and leaped over the brackish trickle of water oozing listlessly out of the culvert which poked out of the cinders. Beyond this small boggy area was the sandy, trash-littered verge of the dump.

There was a six-foot security fence surrounding it. Every twenty feet weather-faded signs were posted. They said:

> CASTLE ROCK DUMP
>
> HOURS 4-8 P.M.
>
> CLOSED MONDAYS
>
> TRESPASSING STRICTLY FORBIDDEN

We climbed to the top of the fence, swung over, and jumped down. Teddy and Vern led the way toward the well, which you tapped with an old-fashioned pump—the kind from which you had to call the water with elbow-grease. There was a Crisco can filled with water next to the pump handle, and the great sin was to forget to leave it filled for the next guy to come along. The iron handle stuck off at an angle, looking a one-winged bird that was trying to fly. It had once been green, but almost all of the paint had been rubbed off by the thousands of hands that had worked that handle since 1940.

The dump is one of my strongest memories of Castle Rock. It always reminds me of the surrealist painters when I think of it—those fellows who were always painting pictures of clockfaces lying limply in the crotches of trees or Victorian living rooms standing in the middle of the Sahara or steam engines coming out of fireplaces. To my child's eye, *nothing* in the Castle Rock Dump looked as if it really belonged there.

We had entered from the back. If you came from the front, a wide dirt road came in through the gate, broadened out into a semicircular area that had been bulldozed as flat as a dirt landing-strip, and then ended abruptly at the edge of the dumping-pit. The pump (Teddy and Vern were currently standing there and squabbling about who was going to prime it) was at the back of this great pit. It was maybe eighty feet deep and filled with all the American things that get empty, wear out, or just don't work anymore. There was so much stuff that my eyes hurt just looking at it—or maybe it was your brain that actually hurt, because it could never quite decide what your eye should stop on. Then your eye *would* stop, or be stopped, by something that seemed as out of place as those limp clockfaces or the living room in the desert. A brass bedstead leaning drunkenly in the sun. A little girl's dolly looking amazedly between her thighs as she gave birth to stuffing. An overturned Studebaker automobile with its chrome bullet nose glittering in the sun like some Buck Rogers missile. One of those giant water bottles they have in office buildings, transformed by the summer sun into a hot, blazing sapphire.

There was plenty of wildlife there, too, although it wasn't the kind you see in the Walt Disney nature films or at those tame zoos where you can pet the animals. Plump rats, woodchucks grown sleek and lumbering on such rich chow as rotting hamburger and maggoty vegetables, seagulls by the thousands, and stalking among the gulls like thoughtful, introspective ministers, an occasional huge crow. It was also the place where the town's stray dogs came for a meal when they couldn't find any trashcans to knock over or any deer to run. They were a miserable, ugly-tempered, mongrel lot; slat-sided and grinning bitterly, they would attack each other over a flyblown piece of bologna or a pile of chicken guts fuming in the sun.

But these dogs never attacked Milo Pressman, the dump-keeper, because Milo was never without Chopper at his heel. Chopper was—at least until Joe Camber's dog Cujo went rabid twenty years later—the most feared and least seen dog in Castle Rock. He was the meanest dog for forty miles around (or so we heard), and ugly enough to stop a striking clock. The kids whispered legends about Chopper's meanness. Some said he was half German shepherd, some said he was mostly boxer, and a kid from Castle View with the unfortunate name of Harry Horr claimed that Chopper was a Doberman pinscher whose vocal cords had been surgically removed so you couldn't hear him when he was on the attack. There were other kids who claimed Chopper was a maniacal Irish wolfhound and Milo Pressman fed him a special mixture of Gaines Meal and chicken blood. These same kids claimed that Milo didn't dare take Chopper out of his shack unless the dog was hooded like a hunting falcon.

The most common story was that Pressman had trained Chopper not just to sic but to sic specific *parts* of the human anatomy. Thus an unfortunate kid who had illegally scaled the dump fence to pick up illicit treasures might hear Milo Pressman cry: "Chopper! Sic! Hand!" And Chopper would grab that hand and hold on, ripping skin and tendons, powdering bones between his slavering jaws, until Milo told him to quit. It was rumored that Chopper could take an ear, an eye, a foot, or a leg . . . and that a second offender who was surprised by Milo and the ever-loyal Chopper would hear the dread cry: "Chopper! Sic! Balls!" And that kid would be a soprano for the rest of his life. Milo himself was more commonly seen and thus more commonly regarded. He was just a half-bright working joe who supplemented his small town salary by fixing things people threw away and selling them around town.

There was no sign of either Milo or Chopper today.

Chris and I watched Vern prime the pump while Teddy worked the handle frantically. At last he was rewarded with a flood of clear water. A moment later both of them had their heads under the trough, Teddy still pumping away a mile a minute.

"Teddy's crazy," I said softly.

"Oh yeah," Chris said matter-of-factly. "He won't live to be twice the age he is now, I bet. His dad burnin his ears like that. That's what did it. He's crazy to dodge trucks the way he does. He can't see worth a shit, glasses or no glasses."

"You remember that time in the tree?"

"Yeah."

The year before, Teddy and Chris had been climbing the big pine tree behind my house. They were almost to the top and Chris said they couldn't go any further because all of the branches up there were rotten. Teddy got that crazy, stubborn look on his face and said fuck that, he had pine tar all over his hands and he was gonna go up until he could touch the top. Nothing Chris said could talk him out of it. So up he went, and he actually made it—he only weighed seventy-five pounds or so, remember. He stood there, clutching the top of the pine in one tar-gummy hand, shouting that he was king of the world or some stupid thing like that, and then there was a sickening, rotted crack as the branch he was standing on gave way and he plummeted. What happened next was one of those things that make you sure there must be a God. Chris reached out, purely on reflex, and what he caught was a fistful of Teddy Duchamp's hair. And although his wrist swelled up fat and he was unable to use his right hand very well for almost two weeks, Chris held him until Teddy, screaming and cursing, got his foot on a live branch thick enough to support his weight. Except for Chris's blind grab, he would have turned and crashed and smashed all the way to the foot of the tree, a hundred and twenty feet below. When they got down, Chris was gray-faced and almost puking with the fear reaction. And Teddy wanted to fight him for pulling his hair. They would have gone at it, too, if I hadn't been there to make peace.

"I dream about that every now and then," Chris said, and looked at me with strangely defenseless eyes. "Except in this dream I have, I always miss him. I just get a couple of hairs and Teddy screams and down he goes. Weird, huh?"

"Weird," I agreed, and for just one moment we looked in each other's eyes and saw some of the true things that made us friends. Then we looked away again and watched Teddy and Vern throwing water at each other, screaming and laughing and calling each other pussies.

"Yeah, but you didn't miss him," I said. "Chris Chambers never misses, am I right?"

"Not even when the ladies leave the seat down," he said. He winked at me, formed an O with his thumb and forefinger, and spat a neat white bullet through it.

"Eat me raw, Chambers," I said.

"Through a Flavor Straw," he said, and we grinned at each other.

Vern yelled: *"Come on and get your water before it runs back down the pipe!"*

"Race you," Chris said.

"In this heat? You're off your gourd."

"Come on," he said, still grinning. "On my go."

"Okay."

"Go!"

We raced, our sneakers digging up the hard, sunbaked dirt,

our torsos leaning out ahead of our flying bluejeaned legs, our fists doubled. It was a dead heat, with both Vern on Chris's side and Teddy on mine holding up their middle fingers at the same moment. We collapsed laughing in the still, smoky odor of the place, and Chris tossed Vern his canteen. When it was full, Chris and I went to the pump and first Chris pumped for me and then I pumped for him, the shocking cold water sluicing off the soot and the heat all in a flash, sending our suddenly freezing scalps four months ahead into January. Then I re-filled the lard can and we all walked over to sit down in the shade of the dump's only tree, a stunted ash forty feet from Milo Pressman's tarpaper shack. The tree was hunched slightly to the west, as if what it really wanted to do was pick up its roots the way an old lady would pick up her skirts and just get the hell out of the dump.

"The most!" Chris said, laughing, tossing his tangled hair back from his brow.

"A blast," I said, nodding, still laughing myself.

"This is really a good time," Vern said simply, and he didn't just mean being off-limits inside the dump, or fudging our folks, or going on a hike up the railroad tracks into Harlow; he meant those things but it seems to me now that there was more, and that we all knew it. Everything was there and around us. We knew exactly who we were and exactly where we were going. It was grand.

We sat under the tree for awhile, shooting the shit like we always did—who had the best ballteam (still the Yankees with Mantle and Maris, of course), what was the best car ('55 Thunderbird, with Teddy holding out stubbornly for the '58 Corvette), who was the toughest guy in Castle Rock who wasn't in our gang (we all agreed it was Jamie Gallant, who gave Mrs. Ewing the finger and then sauntered out of her class with his hands in his pockets while she shouted at him), the best

TV show (either *The Untouchables* or *Peter Gunn*—both Robert Stack as Eliot Ness and Craig Stevens as Gunn were cool), all that stuff.

It was Teddy who first noticed that the shade of the ash tree was getting longer and asked me what time it was. I looked at my watch and was surprised to see it was quarter after two.

"Hey man," Vern said. "Somebody's got to go for provisions. Dump opens at four. I don't want to still be here when Milo and Chopper make the scene."

Even Teddy agreed. He wasn't afraid of Milo, who had a pot belly and was at least forty, but every kid in Castle Rock squeezed his balls between his legs when Chopper's name was mentioned.

"Okay," I said. "Odd man goes?"

"That's you, Gordie," Chris said, smiling. "Odd as a cod."

"So's your mother," I said, and gave them each a coin. "Flip."

Four coins glittered up into the sun. Four hands snatched them from the air. Four flat smacks on four grimy wrists. We uncovered. Two heads and two tails. We flipped again and this time all four of us had tails.

"Oh Jesus, that's a goocher," Vern said, not telling us anything we didn't know. Four heads, or a moon, was supposed to be extraordinarily good luck. Four tails was a goocher, and that meant very bad luck.

"Fuck that shit," Chris said. "It doesn't mean anything. Go again."

"No, man," Vern said earnestly. "A goocher, that's really bad. You remember when Clint Bracken and those guys got wiped out on Sirois Hill in Durham? Billy tole me they was flippin for beers and they came up a goocher just before they got into the car. And bang! they all get fuckin totalled. I don't like that. Sincerely."

"Nobody believes that crap about moons and goochers,"

Teddy said impatiently. "It's baby stuff, Vern. You gonna flip or not?"

Vern flipped, but with obvious reluctance. This time he, Chris, and Teddy all had tails. I was showing Thomas Jefferson on a nickel. And I was suddenly scared. It was as if a shadow had crossed some inner sun. They still had a goocher, the three of them, as if dumb fate had pointed at them a second time. Abruptly I thought of Chris saying: *I just get a couple of hairs and Teddy screams and down he goes. Weird, huh?*

Three tails, one head.

Then Teddy was laughing his crazy, cackling laugh and pointing at me and the feeling was gone.

"I heard that only fairies laugh like that," I said, and gave him the finger.

"Eeee-eeee-eeee, Gordie," Teddy laughed. "Go get the provisions, you fuckin morphadite."

I wasn't really sorry to be going. I was rested up and didn't mind going down the road to the Florida Market.

"Don't call me any of your mother's pet names," I said to Teddy.

"Eeee-eee-eeee, what a fuckin wet you are, Lachance."

"Go on, Gordie," Chris said. "We'll wait over by the tracks."

"You guys better not go without me," I said.

Vern laughed. "Goin without you'd be like goin with Slitz instead of Budweiser's, Gordie."

"Ah, shut up."

They chanted together: "I don't shut up, I *grow* up. And when I look at you I *throw* up."

"Then your mother goes around the corner and licks it up," I said, and hauled ass out of there, giving them the finger over my shoulder as I went. I never had any friends later on like the ones I had when I was twelve. Jesus, did you?

12

Different strokes for different folks, they say now, and that's cool. So if I say *summer* to you, you get one set of private, personal images that are all the way different from mine. That's cool. But for me, *summer* is always going to mean running down the road to the Florida Market with change jingling in my pockets, the temperature in the gay nineties, my feet dressed in Keds. The word conjures an image of the GS&WM railroad tracks running into a perspective-point in the distance, burnished so white under the sun that when you closed your eyes you could still see them there in the dark, only blue instead of white.

But there was more to that summer than our trip across the river to look for Ray Brower, although that looms the largest. Sounds of The Fleetwoods singing, "Come Softly to Me" and Robin Luke singing "Susie Darlin" and Little Anthony popping the vocal on "I Ran All the Way Home." Were they all hits in that summer of 1960? Yes and no. Mostly yes. In the long purple evenings when rock and roll from WLAM blurred into night baseball from WCOU, time shifted. I think it was all 1960 and that the summer went on for a space of years, held magically intact in a web of sounds: the sweet hum of crickets, the machine-gun roar of playing-cards riffling against the spokes of some kid's bicycle as he pedaled home for a late supper of cold cuts and iced tea, the flat Texas voice of Buddy Knox singing "Come along and be my party doll, and I'll make love to you, to you," and the baseball announcer's voice mingling with the song and with the smell of freshly cut grass: "Count's three and two now. Whitey Ford leans over . . . shakes off the sign . . . now he's got it . . . Ford pauses . . . pitches . . . *and there it goes! Williams got all of that one! Kiss it goodbye! RED SOX LEAD, THREE TO ONE!*" Was Ted Williams still playing for the Red Sox in 1960? You bet your ass he was—.316 for my man Ted. I remember that very clearly. Baseball had become important to me in the last couple of years, ever since I'd had to face the knowledge that baseball players were as much flesh and blood as I was. That knowledge came when Roy Campanella's car overturned and the papers screamed mortal news from the front pages: his career was done, he was going to sit in a wheelchair for the rest of his life. How that came back to me, with that same sickening mortal thud, when I sat down to this typewriter one morning two years ago, turned on the radio, and heard that Thurman Munson had died while trying to land his airplane.

There were movies to go see at the Gem, which has long since been torn down; science fiction movies like *Gog* with Richard Egan and westerns with Audie Murphy (Teddy saw every movie Audie Murphy made at least three times; he believed Murphy was almost a god) and war movies with John Wayne. There were games and endless bolted meals, lawns to mow, places to run to, walls to pitch pennies against, people to clap you on the back. And now I sit here trying to look through an IBM keyboard and see that time, trying to recall the best and the worst of that green and brown summer, and I can almost feel the skinny, scabbed boy still buried in this advancing body and hear those sounds. But the apotheosis of the memory and the time is Gordon Lachance running down the road to the Florida Market with change in his pockets and sweat running down his back.

I asked for three pounds of hamburger and got some hamburger rolls, four bottles of Coke and a two-cent churchkey to open them with. The owner, a man named George Dusset, got the meat and then leaned by his cash register, one hammy hand planted on the counter by the big bottle of hardcooked eggs, a toothpick in his mouth, his huge beer belly rounding his white tee-shirt like a sail filled with a good wind. He stood right there as I shopped, making sure I didn't try to hawk anything. He didn't say a word until he was weighing up the hamburger.

"I know you. You're Denny Lachance's brother. Ain't you?" The toothpick journeyed from one corner of his mouth to the other, as if on ball bearings. He reached behind the cash register, picked up a bottle of S'OK cream soda, and chugged it.

"Yes, sir. But Denny, he—"

"Yeah, I know. That's a sad thing, kid. The Bible says: 'In the midst of life, we are in death.' Did you know that? Yuh. I lost a brother in Korea. You look just like Denny, people ever tell you that? Yuh. Spitting image."

"Yes, sir, sometimes," I said glumly.

"I remember the year he was All-Conference. Halfback, he played. Yuh. Could he run? Father God and Sonny Jesus! You're probably too young to remember." He was looking over my head, out through the screen door and into the blasting heat, as if he were having a beautiful vision of my brother.

"I remember. Uh, Mr. Dusset?"

"What, kid?" His eyes were still misty with memory; the toothpick trembled a little between his lips.

"Your thumb is on that scales."

"*What?*" He looked down, astounded, to where the ball of his thumb was pressed firmly on the white enamel. If I hadn't moved away from him a little bit when he started talking about Dennis, the ground meat would have hidden it. "Why, so it is. Yuh. I guess I just got thinkin about your brother, God love him." George Dusset signed a cross on himself. When he took his thumb off the scales, the needle sprang back six ounces. He patted a little more meat on top and then did the package up with white butcher's paper.

"Okay," he said past the toothpick. "Let's see what we got

here. Three pounds of hamburg, that's a dollar forty-four. Hamburg rolls, that's twenty-seven. Four sodas, forty cents. One churchkey, two pence. Comes to . . ." He added it up on the bag he was going to put the stuff in. "Two-twenty-nine."

"Thirteen," I said.

He looked up at me very slowly, frowning. "Huh?"

"Two-thirteen. You added it wrong."

"Kid, are you—"

"You added it wrong," I said. "First you put your thumb on the scales and then you overcharged on the groceries, Mr. Dusset. I was gonna throw some Hostess Twinkies on top of that order but now I guess I won't." I spanged two dollars and thirteen cents down on the Schlitz placemat in front of him.

He looked at the money, then at me. The frown was now tremendous, the lines on his face as deep as fissures. "What are you, kid?" he said in a low voice that was ominously confidential. "Are you some kind of smartass?"

"No, sir," I said. "But you ain't gonna jap me and get away with it. What would your mother say if she knew you was japping little kids?"

He thrust our stuff into the paper bag with quick stiff movements, making the Coke bottles clink together. He thrust the bag at me roughly, not caring if I dropped it and broke the sodas or not. His swarthy face was flushed and dull, the frown now frozen in place. "Okay, kid. Here you go. Now what you do is you get the Christ out of my store. I see you in here again and I going to throw you out, me. Yuh. Smartass little sonofawhore."

"I won't come in again," I said, walking over to the screen door and pushing it open. The hot afternoon buzzed somnolently along its appointed course outside, sounding green and brown and full of silent light. "Neither will none of my friends. I guess I got fifty or so."

"Your brother wasn't no smartass!" George Dusset yelled.

"Fuck you!" I yelled, and ran like hell down the road.

I heard the screen door bang open like a gunshot and his bull roar came after me: *"If you ever come in here again I'll fat your lip for you, you little punk!"*

I ran until I was over the first hill, scared and laughing to myself, my heart beating out a triphammer pulse in my chest. Then I slowed to a fast walk, looking back over my shoulder every now and then to make sure he wasn't going to take after me in his car, or anything.

He didn't, and pretty soon I got to the dump gate. I put the bag inside my shirt, climbed the gate, and monkeyed down the other side. I was halfway across the dump area when I saw something I didn't like—Milo Pressman's portholed '56 Buick was parked behind his tarpaper shack. If Milo saw me I was going to be in a world of hurt. As yet there was no sign of either him or the infamous Chopper, but all at once the chain-link fence at the back of the dump seemed very far away. I found myself wishing I'd gone around the outside, but I was now too far into the dump to want to turn around and go back. If Milo saw me climbing the dump fence, I'd probably be in dutch when I got home, but that didn't scare me as much as Milo yelling for Chopper to sic would.

Scary violin music started to play in my head. I kept putting one foot in front of the other, trying to look casual, trying to look as if I belonged here with a paper grocery sack poking out of my shirt, heading for the fence between the dump and the railroad tracks.

I was about fifty feet from the fence and just beginning to think that everything was going to be all right after all when I heard Milo shout: "Hey! Hey, you! Kid! Get away f'n that fence! Get outta here!"

The smart thing to have done would have been to just agree

with the guy and go around, but by then I was so keyed that instead of doing the smart thing I just broke for the fence with a wild yell, my sneakers kicking up dirt. Vern, Teddy, and Chris came out of the underbrush on the other side of the fence and stared anxiously through the chain-link.

"You come back here!" Milo bawled. *"Come back here or I'll sic my dawg on you, goddammit!"*

I did not exactly find that to be the voice of sanity and conciliation, and I ran even faster for the fence, my arms pumping, the brown grocery bag crackling against my skin. Teddy started to laugh his idiotic chortling laugh, *eee-eee-eeee* into the air like some reed instrument being played by a lunatic.

"Go, Gordie! Go!" Vern screamed.

And Milo yelled: "Sic 'im, Chopper! Go get 'im, boy!"

I threw the bag over the fence and Vern elbowed Teddy out of the way to catch it. Behind me I could hear Chopper coming, shaking the earth, blurting fire out of one distended nostril and ice out of the other, dripping sulphur from his champing jaws. I threw myself halfway up the fence with one leap, screaming. I made it to the top in no more than three seconds and simply leaped—I never thought about it, never even looked down to see what I might land on. What I *almost* landed on was Teddy, who was doubled over and laughing like crazy. His glasses had fallen off and tears were streaming out of his eyes. I missed him by inches and hit the clay-gravel embankment just to his left. At the same instant, Chopper hit the chain-link fence behind me and let out a howl of mingled pain and disappointment. I turned around, holding one skinned knee, and got my first look at the famous Chopper— and my first lesson in the vast difference between myth and reality.

Instead of some huge hellhound with red, savage eyes and teeth jutting out of his mouth like straight-pipes from a hotrod, I was looking at a medium-sized mongrel dog that was a perfectly common black and white. He was yapping and jumping fruitlessly, going up on his back legs to paw the fence.

Teddy was now strutting up and down in front of the fence, twiddling his glasses in one hand, and inciting Chopper to ever greater rage.

"Kiss my ass, Choppie!" Teddy invited, spittle flying from his lips. "Kiss my ass! Bite shit!"

He bumped his fanny against the chain-link fence and Chopper did his level best to take Teddy up on his invitation. He got nothing for his pains but a good healthy nose-bump. He began to bark crazily, foam flying from his snout. Teddy kept bumping his rump against the fence and Chopper kept lunging at it, always missing, doing nothing but racking out his nose, which was now bleeding. Teddy kept exhorting him, calling him by the somehow grisly diminutive "Choppie," and Chris and Vern were lying weakly on the embankment, laughing so hard that they could now do little more than wheeze.

And here came Milo Pressman, dressed in sweat-stained fatigues and a New York Giants baseball cap, his mouth drawn down in distracted anger.

"Here, here!" he was yelling. "You boys stop a-teasing that dawg! You hear me? *Stop it right now!*"

"Bite it, Choppie!" Teddy yelled, strutting up and down on our side of the fence like a mad Prussian reviewing his troops. "Come on and sic me! Sic me!"

Chopper went nuts. I mean it sincerely. He ran around in a big circle, yelping and barking and foaming, rear feet spewing up tough little dry clods. He went around about three times, getting his courage up, I guess, and then he launched himself straight at the security fence. He must have been going thirty miles an hour when he hit it, I kid you not—his doggy lips were stretched back from his teeth and his ears were flying in the slipstream. The whole fence made a low, musical sound as the chain-link was not just driven back against the posts but sort of *stretched* back. It was like a zither note—*yimmmmmmmmm.* A strangled yawp came out of Chopper's mouth, both eyes came up blank and he did a totally amazing reverse snap-roll, landing on his back with a solid thump that sent dust puffing up around him. He just lay there for a moment and then he crawled off with his tongue hanging crookedly from the left side of his mouth.

At this, Milo himself went almost berserk with rage. His complexion darkened to a scary plum color—even his scalp was purple under the short hedgehog bristles of his flattop haircut. Sitting stunned in the dirt, both knees of my jeans torn out, my heart still thudding from the nearness of my escape, I thought that Milo looked like a human version of Chopper.

"I know you!" Milo raved. "You're Teddy Duchamp! I know *all* of you! Sonny, I'll beat your ass, teasing my dawg like that!"

"Like to see you try!" Teddy raved right back. "Let's see you climb over this fence and get me, fatass!"

"WHAT? WHAT DID YOU CALL ME?"

"FATASS!" Teddy screamed happily. *"LARD-BUCKET! TUBBAGUTS! COME ON! COME ON!"* He was jumping up and down, fists clenched, sweat flying from his hair. *"TEACH YOU TO SIC YOUR STUPID DOG ON PEOPLE! COME ON! LIKE TO SEE YOU TRY!"*

"You little tin-weasel peckerwood loony's son! I'll see your mother gets an invitation to go down and talk to the judge in court about what you done to my dawg!"

"What did you call me?" Teddy asked hoarsely. He had stopped jumping up and down. His eyes had gone huge and glassy, and his skin was the color of lead.

Milo had called Teddy a lot of things, but he was able to go

67

back and get the one that had struck home with no trouble at all—since then I have noticed again and again what a genius people have for that . . . for finding the loony button down inside and not just pressing it but hammering on the fucker.

"Your dad was a loony," he said, grinning. "Loony up in Togus, that's what. Crazier'n a shithouse rat. Crazier'n a buck with tickwood fever. Nuttier'n a long-tailed cat in a room fulla rockin chairs. Loony. No wonder you're actin the way you are, with a loony for a f—"

"*YOUR MOTHER BLOWS DEAD RATS!*" Teddy screamed. "*AND IF YOU CALL MY DAD A LOONY AGAIN, I'LL FUCKING KILL YOU, YOU COCKSUCKER!*"

"Loony," Milo said smugly. He'd found the button, all right. "Loony's kid, loony's kid, your father's got toys in the attic, kid, tough break."

Vern and Chris had been getting over their laughing fit, perhaps getting ready to appreciate the seriousness of the situation and call Teddy off, but when Teddy told Milo that his mother blew dead rats, they went back into hysterics again, lying there on the bank, rolling from side to side, their feet kicking, holding their bellies. "No more," Chris said weakly. "No more, please, no more, I swear to God I'm gonna *bust!*"

Chopper was walking around in a large, dazed figure-eight behind Milo. He looked like the losing fighter about ten seconds after the ref has ended the match and awarded the winner a TKO. Meanwhile, Teddy and Milo continued their discussion of Teddy's father, standing nose to nose, with the wire fence Milo was too old and too fat to climb between them.

"Don't you say nothing else about my dad! My dad stormed the beach at Normandy, you fucking wet end!"

"Yeah, well, where is he now, you ugly little four-eyed turd? He's up to Togus, ain't he? He's up to Togus because *HE WENT FUCKING SECTION EIGHT!*"

"Okay, that's it," Teddy said. "That's it, that's the end, I'm gonna kill you." He threw himself at the fence and started up.

"You come on and try it, you slimy little bastard." Milo stood back, grinning and waiting.

"No!" I shouted. I got to my feet, grabbed Teddy by the loose seat of his jeans, and pulled him off the fence. We both staggered back and fell over, him on top. He squashed my balls pretty good and I groaned. Nothing hurts like having your balls squashed, you know it? But I kept my arms locked around Teddy's middle.

"Lemme up!" Teddy sobbed, writhing in my arms. "Lemme up, Gordie! Nobody ranks out my old man. *LEMME UP GODDAMMIT LEMME UP!*"

"That's just what he wants!" I shouted in his ear. "He wants to get you over there and beat the piss out of you and then take you to the cops!"

"Huh?" Teddy craned around to look at me, his face dazed.

"Never mind your smartmouth, kid," Milo said, advancing to the fence again with his hands curled into ham-sized fists. "Let'im fight his own battles."

"Sure," I said. "You only outweigh him by five hundred pounds."

"I know you, too," Milo said ominously. "Your name's Lachance." He pointed to where Vern and Chris were finally picking themselves up, still breathing fast from laughing so hard. "And those guys are Chris Chambers and one of those stupid Tessio kids. All your fathers are going to get calls from me, except for the loony up to Togus. You'll go to the 'formatory, every one of you. Juvenile delinquents!"

He stood flat on his feet, big freckled hands held out like a guy who wanted to play One Potato Two Potato, breathing hard, eyes narrow, waiting for us to cry or say we were sorry or maybe give him Teddy so he could feed Teddy to Chopper.

Chris made an O out of his thumb and index finger and spat neatly through it.

Vern hummed and looked at the sky.

Teddy said: "Come on, Gordie. Let's get away from this asshole before I puke."

"Oh, you're gonna get it, you foulmouthed little whoremaster. Wait'll I get you to the Constable."

"We heard what you said about his father," I told him. "We're all witnesses. And you sicced that dog on me. That's against the law."

Milo looked a trifle uneasy. "You was trespassin."

"The hell I was. The dump's public property."

"You climbed the fence."

"Sure I did, after you sicced your dog on me," I said, hoping that Milo wouldn't recall that I'd also climbed the gate to get in. "What'd you think I was gonna do? Stand there and let 'im rip me to pieces? Come on, you guys. Let's go. It stinks around here."

" 'Formatory," Milo promised hoarsely, his voice shaking. "'Formatory for you wiseguys."

"Can't wait to tell the cops how you called a war vet a fuckin loony," Chris called back over his shoulder as we moved away. "What did *you* do in the war, Mr. Pressman?"

"NONE OF YOUR DAMN BUSINESS!" Milo shrieked. *"YOU HURT MY DAWG!"*

"Put it on your t.s. slip and send it to the chaplain," Vern muttered, and then we were climbing the railroad embankment again.

"Come back here!" Milo shouted, but his voice was fainter now and he seemed to be losing interest.

Teddy shot him the finger as we walked away. I looked back over my shoulder when we got to the top of the embankment. Milo was standing there behind the security fence, a big man in a baseball cap with his dog sitting beside him. His fingers were hooked through the small chain-link diamonds as he shouted at us, and all at once I felt very sorry for him— he looked like the biggest third-grader in the world, locked inside the playground by mistake, yelling for someone to come and let him out. He kept on yelling for awhile and then he either gave up or we got out of range. No more was seen or heard of Milo Pressman and Chopper that day.

13

There was some discussion—in righteous tones that were actually kind of forced-sounding—about how we had shown that creepy Milo Pressman we weren't just another bunch of pussies. I told how the guy at the Florida Market had tried to jap us, and then we fell into a gloomy silence, thinking it over.

For my part, I was thinking that maybe there was something to that stupid goocher business after all. Things couldn't have turned out much worse—in fact, I thought, it might be better to just keep going and spare my folks the pain of having one son in the Castle View Cemetery and one in South Windham Boys' Correctional. I had no doubt that Milo would go to the cops as soon as the importance of the dump having been closed at the time of the incident filtered into his thick skull. When that happened, he would realize that I really *had* been trespassing, public property or not. Probably that gave him every right in the world to sic his stupid dog on me. And while Chopper wasn't the hellhound he was cracked up to be, he sure would have ripped the sitdown out of my jeans if I hadn't won the race to the fence. All of it put a big dark crimp in the day. And there was another gloomy idea rolling around inside my head—the idea that this was no lark after all, and maybe we deserved our bad luck. Maybe it was even God warning us to go home. What were we doing, anyway, going to look at some kid that had gotten himself all mashed up by a freight train?

But we were doing it, and none of us wanted to stop.

We had almost reached the trestle which carried the tracks across the river when Teddy burst into tears. It was as if a great inner tidal wave had broken through a carefully constructed set of mental dykes. No bullshit—it was that sudden and that fierce. The sobs doubled him over like punches and he sort of collapsed into a heap, his hands going from his stomach to the mutilated gobs of flesh that were the remains of his ears. He went on crying in hard, violent bursts.

None of us knew what the fuck to do. It wasn't crying like when you got hit by a line drive while you were playing shortstop or smashed on the head playing tackle football on the common or when you fell off your bike. There was nothing physically wrong with him. We walked away a little and watched him, our hands in our pockets.

"Hey, man . . ." Vern said in a very thin voice. Chris and I looked at Vern hopefully. "Hey, man" was always a good start. But Vern couldn't follow it up.

Teddy leaned forward onto the crossties and put a hand over his eyes. Now he looked like he was doing the Allah bit—"Salami, salami, baloney," as Popeye says. Except it wasn't funny.

At last, when the force of his crying had trailed off a little, it was Chris who went to him. He was the toughest guy in our gang (maybe even tougher than Jamie Gallant, I thought privately), but he was also the guy who made the best peace. He had a way about it. I'd seen him sit down on the curb next to a little kid with a scraped knee, a kid he didn't even fucking *know,* and get him talking about something—the Shrine Circus that was coming to town or Huckleberry Hound on TV—

until the kid forgot he was supposed to be hurt. Chris was good at it. He was tough enough to be good at it.

"Lissen, Teddy, what do you care what a fat old pile of shit like him said about your father? Huh? I mean, sincerely! That don't change nothing, does it? What a fat old pile of shit like him says? Huh? Huh? Does it?"

Teddy shook his head violently. It changed nothing. But to hear it spoken of in bright daylight, something he must have gone over and over in his mind while he was lying awake in bed and looking at the moon off-center in one windowpane, something he must have thought about in his slow and broken way until it seemed almost holy, trying to make sense out of it, and then to have it brought home to him that everybody else had merely dismissed his dad as a loony . . . that had rocked him. But it changed nothing. Nothing.

"He still stormed the beach at Normandy, right?" Chris said. He picked up one of Teddy's sweaty, grimy hands and patted it.

Teddy nodded fiercely, crying. Snot was running out of his nose.

"Do you think that pile of shit was at Normandy?"

Teddy shook his head violently. *"Nuh-Nuh-No!"*

"Do you think that guy knows you?"

"Nuh-No! No, b-b-but—"

"Or your father? He one of your father's buddies?"

"NO!" Angry, horrified. The thought. Teddy's chest heaved and more sobs came out of it. He had pushed his hair away from his ears and I could see the round brown plastic button of the hearing aid set in the middle of his right one. The shape of the hearing aid made more sense than the shape of his ear, if you get what I mean.

Chris said calmly: "Talk is cheap."

Teddy nodded, still not looking up.

73

"And whatever's between you and your old man, talk can't change that."

Teddy's head shook without definition, unsure if this was true. Someone had redefined his pain, and redefined it in shockingly common terms. That would

(loony)

have to be examined

(fucking section eight)

later. In depth. On long sleepless nights.

Chris rocked him. "He was ranking you, man," he said in soothing cadences that were almost a lullaby. "He was tryin to rank you over that friggin fence, you know it? No strain, man. No fuckin strain. He don't know nothin about your old man. He don't know nothin but stuff he heard from those rumdums down at The Mellow Tiger. He's just dogshit, man. Right, Teddy? Huh? Right?"

Teddy's crying was down to sniffles. He wiped his eyes, leaving two sooty rings around them, and sat up.

"I'm okay," he said, and the sound of his own voice seemed to convince him. "Yeah, I'm okay." He stood up and put his glasses back on—dressing his naked face, it seemed to me. He laughed thinly and swiped his bare arm across the snot of his upper lip. "Fuckin crybaby, right?"

"No, man," Vern said uncomfortably. "If anyone was rankin out my dad—"

"Then you got to kill em!" Teddy said briskly, almost arrogantly. "Kill their asses. Right, Chris?"

"Right," Chris said amiably, and clapped Teddy on the back. "Right, Gordie?"

"Absolutely," I said, wondering how Teddy could care so much for his dad when his dad had practically killed him, and how I couldn't seem to give much of a shit one way or the other about my own dad, when so far as I could remember, he had never laid a hand on me since I was three and got some bleach from under the sink and started to eat it.

We walked another two hundred yards down the tracks and Teddy said in a quieter voice: "Hey, if I spoiled your good time, I'm sorry. I guess that was pretty stupid shit back there at that fence."

"I ain't sure I want it to be no good time," Vern said suddenly.

Chris looked at him. "You sayin you want to go back, man?"

"No, huh-uh!" Vern's face knotted in thought. "But going to see a dead kid—it shouldn't be a party, maybe. I mean, if you can dig it. I mean . . ." He looked at us rather wildly. "I mean, I could be a little scared. If you get me."

Nobody said anything and Vern plunged on:

"I mean, sometimes I get nightmares. Like . . . aw, you guys remember the time Danny Naughton left that pile of old funnybooks, the ones with the vampires and people gettin cut up and all that shit? Jeezum-crow, I'd wake up in the middle of the night dreamin about some guy hangin in a house with his face all green or somethin, you know, like that, and it seems like there's somethin under the bed and if I dangled a hand over the side, that thing might, you know, grab me . . ."

We all began to nod. We knew about the night shift. I would have laughed then, though, if you had told me that one day not too many years from then I'd parlay all those childhood fears and night-sweats into about a million dollars.

"And I don't dare say anything because my friggin *brother . . .* well, you know Billy . . . he'd broadcast it . . ." He shrugged miserably. "So I'm ascared to look at that kid cause if he's, you know, if he's really *bad . . .*"

I swallowed and glanced at Chris. He was looking gravely at Vern and nodding for him to go on.

"If he's really *bad,*" Vern resumed, "I'll have nightmares about *him* and wake up thinkin it's *him* under my bed, all cut up in a pool of blood like he just came out of one of those Saladmaster gadgets they show on TV, just eyeballs and hair, but *movin* somehow, if you can dig that, *mooovin* somehow, you know, and gettin ready to *grab*—"

"Jesus Christ," Teddy said thickly. "What a fuckin bedtime story."

"Well I can't *help* it," Vern said, his voice defensive. "But I feel like we *hafta* see him, even if there are bad dreams. You know? Like we *hafta*. But . . . but maybe it shouldn't be no good time."

"Yeah," Chris said softly. "Maybe it shouldn't."

Vern said pleadingly: "You won't tell none of the other guys, will you? I don't mean about the nightmares, everybody has those—I mean about wakin up and thinkin there might be somethin under the bed. I'm too fuckin old for the boogeyman."

We all said we wouldn't tell, and a glum silence fell over us again. It was only quarter to three, but it felt much later. It was too hot and too much had happened. We weren't even over into Harlow yet. We were going to have to pick them up and lay them down if we were going to make some real miles before dark.

We passed the railroad junction and a signal on a tall, rusty pole and all of us paused to chuck cinders at the steel flag on top, but nobody hit it. And around three-thirty we came to the Castle River and the GS&WM trestle which crossed it.

14

The river was better than a hundred yards across at that point in 1960; I've been back to look at it since then, and found it had narrowed up quite a bit during the years between. They're always fooling with the river, trying to make it work better for the mills, and they've put in so many dams that it's pretty well tamed. But in those days there were only three dams on the whole length of the river as it ran across New Hampshire and half of Maine. The Castle was still almost free back then, and every third spring it would overflow its banks and cover Route 136 in either Harlow or Danvers Junction or both.

Now, at the end of the driest summer western Maine had seen since the depression, it was still broad. From where we stood on the Castle Rock side, the bulking forest on the Harlow side looked like a different country altogether. The pines and spruces over there were bluish in the heat-haze of the afternoon. The rails went across the water fifty feet up, supported by an underpinning of tarred wooden support posts and crisscrossing beams. The water was so shallow you could look down and see the tops of the cement plugs which had been planted ten feet deep in the riverbed to hold up the trestle.

The trestle itself was pretty chintzy—the rails ran over a long, narrow wooden platform of six-by-fours. There was a four-inch gap between each pair of these beams where you could look all the way down into the water. On the sides, there was no more than eighteen inches between the rail and the edge of the trestle. If a train came, it was maybe enough room to avoid getting plastered . . . but the wind generated by a highballing freight would surely sweep you off to fall to a certain death against the rocks just below the surface of the shallow running water.

Looking at the trestle, we all felt fear start to crawl around in our bellies . . . and mixing uneasily with the fear was the excitement of a boss dare, a really big one, something you could brag on for weeks after you got home . . . *if* you got home. That queer light was creeping back into Teddy's eyes and I thought he wasn't seeing the GS&WM train trestle at all

but a long sandy beach, a thousand LSTs aground in the foaming waves, ten thousand GIs charging up the sand, combat
boots digging. They were leaping rolls of barbed wire! Tossing
grenades at pillboxes! Overrunning machine-gun nests!

We were standing beside the tracks where the cinders sloped
away toward the river's cut—the place where the embankment stopped and the trestle began. Looking down, I could
see where the slope started to get steep. The cinders gave way
to scraggly, tough-looking bushes and slabs of gray rock. Further down there were a few stunted firs with exposed roots
writhing their way out of fissures in the plates of rock; they
seemed to be looking down at their own miserable reflections
in the running water.

At this point, the Castle River actually looked fairly clean; at
Castle Rock it was just entering Maine's textile-mill belt. But
there were no fish jumping out there, although the river was
clear enough to see bottom—you had to go another ten miles
upstream and toward New Hampshire before you could see any
fish in the Castle. There were no fish, and along the edges of
the river you could see dirty collars of foam around some of the
rocks—the foam was the color of old ivory. The river's smell
was not particularly pleasant, either; it smelled like a laundry
hamper full of mildewy towels. Dragonflies stitched at the surface of the water and laid their eggs with impunity. There were
no trout to eat them. Hell, there weren't even any shiners.

"Man," Chris said softly.

"Come on," Teddy said in that brisk, arrogant way. "Let's
go." He was already edging his way out, walking on the six-
by-fours between the shining rails.

"Say," Vern said uneasily, "any of you guys know when the
next train's due?"

We all shrugged.

I said: "There's the Route 136 bridge . . ."

"Hey, come on, gimme a break!" Teddy cried. "That means walkin five miles down the river on this side and then five miles back up on the other side . . . it'll take us until dark! If we use the trestle, we can get to the same place in *ten minutes*!"

"But if a train comes, there's nowheres to go," Vern said. He wasn't looking at Teddy. He was looking down at the fast, bland river.

"Fuck there isn't!" Teddy said indignantly. He swung over the edge and held one of the wooden supports between the rails. He hadn't gone out very far—his sneakers were almost touching the ground—but the thought of doing that same thing above the middle of the river with a fifty-foot drop beneath and a train bellowing by just over my head, a train that would probably be dropping some nice hot sparks into my hair and down the back of my neck . . . none of that actually made me feel like Queen for a Day.

"See how easy it is?" Teddy said. He dropped to the embankment, dusted his hands, and climbed back up beside us.

"You tellin me you're gonna hang on that way if it's a two-hundred-car freight?" Chris asked. "Just sorta hang there by your hands for five or ten minutes?"

"You chicken?" Teddy shouted.

"No, just askin what you'd do," Chris said, grinning. "Peace, man."

"Go around if you want to!" Teddy brayed. "Who gives a fuck? I'll wait for you! I'll take a *nap*!"

"One train already went by," I said reluctantly. "And there probably isn't any more than one, two trains a day that go through Harlow. Look at this." I kicked the weeds growing up through the railroad ties with one sneaker. There were no weeds growing between the tracks which ran between Castle Rock and Lewiston.

"There. See?" Teddy triumphant.

"But still, there's a *chance*," I added.

"Yeah," Chris said. He was looking only at me, his eyes sparkling. "Dare you, Lachance."

"Dares go first"

"Okay," Chris said. He widened his gaze to take in Teddy and Vern. "Any pussies here?"

"*NO!*" Teddy shouted.

Vern cleared his throat, croaked, cleared it again, and said "No" in a very small voice. He smiled a weak, sick smile.

"Okay," Chris said . . . but we hesitated for a moment, even Teddy, looking warily up and down the tracks. I knelt down and took one of the steel rails firmly in my hand, never minding that it was almost hot enough to blister the skin. The rail was mute.

"Okay," I said, and as I said it some guy pole-vaulted in my stomach. He dug his pole all the way into my balls, it felt like, and ended up sitting astride my heart.

We went out onto the trestle single file: Chris first, then Teddy, then Vern, and me playing tail-end Charlie because I was the one who said dares go first. We walked on the platform crossties between the rails, and you had to look at your feet whether you were scared of heights or not. A misstep and you would go down to your crotch, probably with a broken ankle to pay.

The embankment dropped away beneath me, and every step further out seemed to seal our decision more firmly . . . and to make it feel more suicidally stupid. I stopped to look up when I saw the rocks giving way to water far beneath me. Chris and Teddy were a long way ahead, almost out over the middle, and Vern was tottering slowly along behind them, peering studiously down at his feet. He looked like an old lady trying out stilts with his head poked downward, his back hunched, his arms held out for balance. I looked back over my shoulder. Too far, man. I had to keep going now, and not only because a train might come. If I went back, I'd be a pussy for life.

So I got walking again. After looking down at that endless series of crossties for awhile, with a glimpse of running water between each pair, I started to feel dizzy and disoriented. Each time I brought my foot down, part of my brain assured me it was going to plunge through into space, even though I could see it was not.

I became acutely aware of all the noises inside me and outside me, like some crazy orchestra tuning up to play. The steady thump of my heart, the bloodbeat in my ears like a drum being played with brushes, the creak of sinews like the strings of a violin that has been tuned radically upward, the steady hiss of the river, the hot hum of a locust digging into tight bark, the monotonous cry of a chickadee, and somewhere, far away, a barking dog. Chopper, maybe. The mildewy smell of the Castle River was strong in my nose. The long muscles in my thighs were trembling. I kept thinking how much safer it would be (probably faster, as well) if I just got down on my hands and knees and scuttered along that way. But I wouldn't do that—none of us would. If the Saturday matinee movies down to the Gem had taught us anything, it was that Only Losers Crawl. It was one of the central tenets of the Gospel According to Hollywood. Good guys walk firmly upright, and if your sinews are creaking like overtimed violin strings because of the adrenaline rush going on in your body, and if the long muscles in your thighs are trembling for the same reason, why, so be it.

I had to stop in the middle of the trestle and look up at the sky for awhile. That dizzy feeling had been getting worse. I saw phantom crossties—they seemed to float right in front of my nose. Then they faded out and I began to feel okay again. I looked ahead and saw I had almost caught up with Vern, who was slowpoking along worse than ever. Chris and Teddy were almost all the way across.

And although I've since written seven books about people who can do such exotic things as read minds and precognit the future, that was when I had my first and last psychic flash. I'm sure that's what it was; how else to explain it? I squatted and made a fist around the rail on my left. It thrummed in my hand. It was thrumming so hard that it was like gripping a bundle of deadly metallic snakes.

You've heard it said "His bowels turned to water"? I know what that phrase means—*exactly* what it means. It may be the most accurate cliché ever coined. I've been scared since, badly scared, but I've never been as scared as I was in that moment, holding that hot live rail. It seemed that for a moment all my works below throat level just went limp and lay there in an internal faint. A thin stream of urine ran listlessly down the inside of one thigh. My mouth opened. I didn't open it, it opened by itself, the jaw dropping like a trapdoor from which the hingepins had suddenly been removed. My tongue was plastered suffocatingly against the roof of my mouth. All my muscles were locked. That was the worst. My works went limp but my muscles were in a kind of dreadful lockbolt and I couldn't move at all. It was only for a moment, but in the subjective timestream, it seemed forever.

All sensory input became intensified, as if some power-surge had occurred in the electrical flow of my brain, cranking everything up from a hundred and ten volts to two-twenty. I could hear a plane passing in the sky somewhere near and had time to wish I was on it, just sitting in a window seat with a Coke in my hand and gazing idly down at the shining line of a river whose name I did not know. I could see every little splinter and gouge in the tarred crosstie I was squatting on. And out of the corner of my eye I could see the rail itself with my

hand still clutched around it, glittering insanely. The vibration from that rail sank so deeply into my hand that when I
took it away it still vibrated, the nerve-endings kicking each
other over again and again, tingling the way a hand or foot
tingles when it has been asleep and is starting to wake up. I
could taste my saliva, suddenly all electric and sour and thick-
ened to curds along my gums. And worst, somehow most horrible of all, I couldn't *hear* the train yet, could not know if it
was rushing at me from ahead or behind, or how close it was.
It was invisible. It was unannounced, except for that shaking
rail. There was only that to advertise its imminent arrival. An
image of Ray Brower, dreadfully mangled and thrown into a
ditch somewhere like a ripped-open laundry bag, reeled before
my eyes. We would join him, or at least Vern and I would, or
at least I would. We had invited ourselves to our own funerals.

The last thought broke the paralysis and I shot to my feet.
I probably would have looked like a jack-in-the-box to anyone
watching, but to myself I felt like a boy in underwater slow
motion, shooting up not through five feet of air but rather up
through five hundred feet of water, moving slowly, moving
with a dreadful languidness as the water parted grudgingly.

But at last I did break the surface.

I screamed: *"TRAIN!"*

The last of the paralysis fell from me and I began to run.

Vern's head jerked back over his shoulder. The surprise that
distorted his face was almost comically exaggerated, written
as large as the letters in a Dick and Jane primer. He saw me
break into my clumsy, shambling run, dancing from one horribly high crosstie to the next, and knew I wasn't joking. He
began to run himself.

Far ahead, I could see Chris stepping off the ties and onto
the solid safe embankment and I hated him with a sudden
bright green hate as juicy and as bitter as the sap in an April

leaf. He was safe. *That* fucker was *safe.* I watched him drop to his knees and grab a rail.

My left foot almost slipped into the yaw beneath me. I flailed with my arms, my eyes as hot as ball bearings in some runaway piece of machinery, got my balance, and ran on. Now I was right behind Vern. We were past the halfway point and for the first time I heard the train. It was coming from behind us, coming from the Castle Rock side of the river. It was a low rumbling noise that began to rise slightly and sort itself into the diesel thrum of the engine and the higher, more sinister sound of big grooved wheels turning heavily on the rails.

"Awwwwwwww, *shit!*" Vern screamed.

"Run, you pussy!" I yelled, and thumped him on the back.

"I can't! I'll fall!"

"Run faster!"

"AWWWWWWWWW-SHIT!"

But he ran faster, a shambling scarecrow with a bare, sunburnt back, the collar of his shirt swinging and dangling below his butt. I could see the sweat standing out on his peeling shoulder-blades, standing out in perfect little beads. I could see the fine down on the nape of his neck. His muscles clenched and loosened, clenched and loosened, clenched and loosened. His spine stood out in a series of knobs, each knob casting its own crescent-shaped shadow—I could see that these knobs grew closer together as they approached his neck. He was still holding his bedroll and I was still holding mine. Vern's feet thudded on the crossties. He almost missed one, lunged forward with his arms out, and I whacked him on the back again to keep him going.

"Gordeee I can't AWWWWWWWWWW-SHEEEEEEYIT—"

"*RUN FASTER, DICKFACE!*" I bellowed and was I *enjoying* this?

Yeah—in some peculiar, self-destructive way that I have experienced since only when completely and utterly drunk,

I was. I was driving Vern Tessio like a drover getting a particularly fine cow to market. And maybe he was enjoying his own fear in that same way, bawling like that self-same cow, hollering and sweating, his ribcage rising and falling like the bellows of a blacksmith on a speed-trip, clumsily keeping his footing, lurching ahead.

The train was very loud now, its engine deepening to a steady rumble. Its whistle sounded as it crossed the junction point where we had paused to chuck cinders at the rail-flag. I had finally gotten my hellhound, like it or not. I kept waiting for the trestle to start shaking under my feet. When that happened, it would be right behind us.

"GO FASTER, VERN! FAAASTER!"

"Oh Gawd Gordie oh Gawd Gordie oh Gawd *AWWWW-WWW-SHEEEEYIT!*"

The freight's electric horn suddenly spanked the air into a hundred pieces with one long loud blast, making everything you ever saw in a movie or a comic book or one of your own daydreams fly apart, letting you know what both the heroes and the cowards really heard when death flew at them:

WHHHHHHHONNNNNNNK! WHHHHHHHHONNNN-NNNNK!

And then Chris was below us and to the right, and Teddy was behind him, his glasses flashing back arcs of sunlight, and they were both mouthing a single word and the word was *jump!* but the train had sucked all the blood out of the word, leaving only its shape in their mouths. The trestle began to shake as the train charged across it. We jumped.

Vern landed full-length in the dust and the cinders and I landed right beside him, almost on top of him. I never did see that train, nor do I know if its engineer saw us—when I mentioned the possibility that he hadn't seen us to Chris a couple of years later, he said: "They don't blow the horn like that just for chucks, Gordie." But he *could* have; he could have been blowing it just for the hell of it. I suppose. Right then, such fine points didn't much matter. I clapped my hands over my ears and dug my face into the hot dirt as the freight went by, metal squalling against metal, the air buffeting us. I had no urge to look at it. It was a long freight but I never looked at all. Before it had passed completely, I felt a warm hand on my neck and knew it was Chris's.

When it was gone—when I was *sure* it was gone—I raised my head like a soldier coming out of his foxhole at the end of a day-long artillery barrage. Vern was still plastered into the dirt, shivering. Chris was sitting cross-legged between us, one hand on Vern's sweaty neck, the other still on mine.

When Vern finally sat up, shaking all over and licking his lips compulsively, Chris said: "What you guys think if we drink those Cokes? Could anybody use one besides me?"

We all thought we could use one.

15

About a quarter of a mile along on the Harlow side, the GS&WM tracks plunged directly into the woods. The heavily wooded land sloped down to a marshy area. It was full of mosquitoes almost as big as fighter-planes, but it was cool . . . blessedly cool.

We sat down in the shade to drink our Cokes. Vern and I threw our shirts over our shoulders to keep the bugs off, but Chris and Teddy just sat naked to the waist, looking as cool and collected as two Eskimos in an icehouse. We hadn't been there five minutes when Vern had to go off into the bushes and take a squat, which led to a good deal of joking and elbowing when he got back.

"Train scare you much, Vern?"

"No," Vern said. "I was gonna squat when we got acrosst, anyway, I *hadda* take a squat, you know?"

"*Verrrrrrrn?*" Chris and Teddy chorused.

"Come on, you guys, I *did.* Sincerely."

"Then you won't mind if we examine the seat of your Jockeys for Hershey-squirts, willya?" Teddy asked, and Vern laughed, finally understanding that he was getting ribbed.

"Go screw."

Chris turned to me. "That train scare you, Gordie?"

"Nope," I said, and sipped my Coke.

"Not much, you sucker." He punched my arm.

"Sincerely! I wasn't scared at all."

"Yeah? You wasn't scared?" Teddy was looking me over carefully.

"No. I was fuckin *petrified.*"

This slew all of them, even Vern, and we laughed long and hard. Then we just lay back, not goofing anymore, just drinking our Cokes and being quiet. My body felt warm, exercised, at peace with itself. Nothing in it was working crossgrain to anything else. I was alive and glad to be. Everything seemed to stand out with a special dearness, and although I never could have said that out loud I didn't think it mattered—maybe that sense of dearness was something I wanted just for myself.

I think I began to understand a little bit that day what makes men become daredevils. I paid twenty dollars to watch Evel Kneivel attempt his jump over the Snake River Canyon a couple of years ago and my wife was horrified. She told me that if I'd been born a Roman I would have been right there in the Colosseum, munching grapes and watching as the lions disemboweled the Christians. She was wrong, although it was hard for me to explain why (and, really, I think *she* thought I was just jiving her). I didn't cough up that twenty to watch the man die on coast-to-coast closed-circuit TV, although I was quite sure that was exactly what was going to happen. I went because of the shadows that are always somewhere behind our eyes, because of what Bruce Springsteen calls the darkness on the edge of town in one of his songs, and at one time or another I think everyone wants to dare that darkness in spite of the jalopy bodies that some joker of a God gave us human beings. No . . . not in *spite* of our jalopy bodies but *because* of them.

"Hey, tell that story," Chris said suddenly, sitting up.

"What story?" I asked, although I guess I knew.

I always felt uncomfortable when the talk turned to my stories, although all of them seemed to like them—wanting to tell stories, even wanting to write them down . . . that was just peculiar enough to be sort of cool, like wanting to grow up to be a sewer inspector or a Grand Prix mechanic. Richie Jenner, a kid who hung around with us until his family moved to Nebraska in 1959, was the first one to find out that I wanted to be a writer when I grew up, that I wanted to do that for my full-time job. We were up in my room, just fooling around, and he found a bunch of handwritten pages under the comic books in a carton in my closet. What's *this?* Richie asks. Nothin, I say, and try to grab them back. Richie held the pages up out of reach . . . and I must admit that I didn't try very *hard* to get them back. I wanted him to read them and at the same time I didn't—an uneasy mix of pride and shyness that has never changed in me very much when someone asks to look. The act of writing itself is done in secret, like masturbation—oh, I have one friend who has done things like write stories in the display windows of bookshops and department stores, but this is a man who is nearly crazy with courage, the kind of man you'd like to have with you if you just happened to fall down with a heart attack in a city where no one knew you. For me, it always wants to be sex and always falls short—

it's always that adolescent handjob in the bathroom with the door locked.

Richie sat right there on the end of my bed for most of the afternoon reading his way through the stuff I had been doing, most of it influenced by the same sort of comic books as the ones that had given Vern nightmares. And when he was done, Richie looked at me in a strange new way that made me feel very peculiar, as if he had been forced to re-appraise my whole personality. He said: You're pretty good at this. Why don't you show these to Chris? I said no, I wanted it to be a secret, and Richie said: Why? It ain't pussy. You ain't no queer. I mean, it ain't *poetry.*

Still, I made him promise not to tell anybody about my stories and of course he did and it turned out most of them liked to read the stuff I wrote, which was mostly about getting burned alive or some crook coming back from the dead and slaughtering the jury that had condemned him in Twelve Interesting Ways or a maniac that went crazy and chopped a lot of people into veal cutlets before the hero, Curt Cannon, "cut the subhuman, screeching madman to pieces with round after round from his smoking .45 automatic."

In my stories, there were always rounds. *Never* bullets.

For a change of pace, there were the Le Dio stories. Le Dio was a town in France, and during 1942, a grim squad of tired American dogfaces were trying to retake it from the Nazis (this was two years before I discovered that the Allies didn't land in France until 1944). They went on trying to retake it, fighting their way from street to street, through about forty stories which I wrote between the ages of nine and fourteen. Teddy was absolutely mad for the Le Dio stories, and I think I wrote the last dozen or so just for him—by then I was heartily sick of Le Dio and writing things like *Mon Dieu* and *Cherchez le Boche!* and *Fermez le porte!* In Le Dio, French peasants were always hissing to GI dogfaces to *Fermez le porte!* But Teddy would hunch over the pages, his eyes big, his brow beaded with sweat, his face twisting. There were times when I could almost hear air-cooled Brownings and whistling 88s going off in his skull. The way he clamored for more Le Dio stories was both pleasing and frightening.

Nowadays writing is my work and the pleasure has diminished a little, and more and more often that guilty, masturbatory pleasure has become associated in my head with the coldly clinical images of artificial insemination: I come according to the rules and regs laid down in my publishing contract. And although no one is ever going to call me the Thomas Wolfe of my generation, I rarely feel like a cheat: I get it off as hard as I can every fucking time. Doing less would, in an odd way, be like going faggot—or what that meant to us back then. What scares me is how often it hurts these days. Back then I was sometimes disgusted by how damned *good* it felt to write. These days I sometimes look at this typewriter and wonder when it's going to run out of good words. I don't want that to happen. I guess I can stay cool as long as I don't run out of good words, you know?

"What's this story?" Vern asked uneasily. "It ain't a horror story, is it, Gordie? I don't think I want to hear no horror stories. I'm not up for that, man."

"No, it ain't a horror," Chris said. "It's really funny. Gross, but funny. Go on, Gordie. Hammer that fucker to us."

"Is it about Le Dio?" Teddy asked.

"No, it ain't about Le Dio, you psycho," Chris said, and rabbit-punched him. "It's about this pie-eatin contest."

"Hey, I didn't even write it down yet," I said.

"Yeah, but tell it."

"You guys want to hear it?"

"Sure," Teddy said. "Boss."

"Well, it's about this made-up town. Gretna, I call it. Gretna, Maine."

"*Gretna?*" Vern said, grinning. "What kind of name is that? There ain't no *Gretna* in Maine."

"Shut up, fool," Chris said. "He just toldja it was made-up, didn't he?"

"Yeah, but *Gretna,* that sounds pretty stupid—"

"Lots of *real* towns sound stupid," Chris said. "I mean, what about *Alfred,* Maine? Or *Saco,* Maine? Or Jerusalem's Lot? Or Castle-fuckin-Rock? There ain't no castle here. *Most* town names are stupid. You just don't think so because you're used to em. Right, Gordie?"

"Sure," I said, but privately I thought Vern was right— Gretna was a pretty stupid name for a town. I just hadn't been able to think of another one. "So anyway, they're having their annual Pioneer Days, just like in Castle Rock—"

"Yeah, Pioneer Days, that's a fuckin *blast,*" Vern said earnestly.

"I put my whole family in that jail on wheels they have, even fuckin Billy. It was only for half an hour and it cost me my whole allowance but it was worth it just to know where that sonofawhore was—"

"Will you shut up and let him tell it?" Teddy hollered.

Vern blinked. "Sure. Yeah. Okay."

"Go on, Gordie," Chris said.

"It's not really much—"

"Naw, we don't expect much from a wet end like you," Teddy said, "but tell it anyway."

I cleared my throat. "So anyway. It's Pioneer Days, and on the last night they have these three big events. There's an egg-roll for the little kids and a sack-race for kids that are like eight or nine, and then there's the pie-eating contest. And the main guy of the story is this fat kid nobody likes named Davie Hogan."

91

"Like Charlie Hogan's brother if he had one," Vern said, and then shrank back as Chris rabbit-punched him again.

"This kid, he's our age, but he's fat. He weighs like one-eighty and he's always gettin beat up and ranked out. And all the kids, instead of callin him Davie, they call him Lard Ass Hogan and rank him out wherever they get the chance."

They nodded respectfully, showing the proper sympathy for Lard Ass, although if such a guy ever showed up in Castle Rock, we all would have been out teasing him and ranking him to the dogs and back.

"So he decides to take revenge because he's, like, fed up, you know? He's only in the pie-eating contest, but that's like the final event during Pioneer Days and everyone really digs it. The prize is five bucks—"

"So he wins it and gives the finger to everybody!" Teddy said. "Boss!"

"No, it's better than that," Chris said. "Just shut up and listen."

"Lard Ass figures to himself, five bucks, what's that? If anybody remembers anything at all in two weeks, it'll just be that fuckin pig Hogan out-ate everybody, well, it figures, let's go over his house and rank the shit out of him, only now we'll call him Pie Ass instead of Lard Ass."

They nodded some more, agreeing that Davie Hogan was a thinking cat. I began to warm to my own story.

"But everybody expects him to enter the contest, you know. Even his mom and dad. Hey, they practically got that five bucks spent for him already."

"Yeah, right," Chris said.

"So he's thinkin about it and hating the whole thing, because being fat isn't really his fault. See, he's got these weird fuckin glands, somethin, and—"

"My cousin's like that!" Vern said excitedly. "Sincerely! She weighs close to three hundred pounds! Supposed to be Hyboid Gland or somethin like that. I dunno about her Hyboid Gland, but what a fuckin blimp, no shit, she looks like a fuckin Thanksgiving turkey, and this one time—"

"Will you shut the fuck *up,* Vern?" Chris cried violently. "For the last time! Honest to God!" He had finished his Coke and now he turned the hourglass-shaped green bottle upside down and brandished it over Vern's head.

"Yeah, right, I'm sorry. Go on, Gordie. It's a swell story."

I smiled. I didn't really mind Vern's interruptions, but of course I couldn't tell Chris that; he was the self-appointed Guardian of Art.

"So he's turnin it over in his mind, you know, the whole week before the contest. At school, kids keep comin up to him and sayin: Hey Lard Ass, how many pies ya gonna eat? Ya gonna eat ten? Twenty? Fuckin *eighty?* And Lard Ass, *he* says: How should I know. I don't even know what *kind* they are. And see, there's quite a bit of interest in the contest because the champ is this grownup whose name is, uh, Bill Traynor, I guess. And this guy Traynor, he ain't even fat. In fact, he's a real stringbean. But he can eat pies like a whiz, and the year before he ate six pies in five minutes."

"*Whole* pies?" Teddy asked, awe-struck.

"Right you are. And Lard Ass, he's the youngest guy to ever be in the contest."

"Go, Lard Ass!" Teddy cried excitedly. "Scoff up those fuckin pies!"

"Tell em about the other guys in it," Chris said.

"Okay. Besides Lard Ass Hogan and Bill Traynor, there was Calvin Spier, the fattest guy in town—he ran the jewelry store—"

"Gretna Jewels," Vern said, and snickered. Chris gave him a black look.

"And then there's this guy who's a disc jockey at a radio station up in Lewiston, he ain't exactly fat but he's sorta chubby, you know. And the last guy was Hubert Gretna the Third, who was the principal of Lard Ass Hogan's school."

"He was eatin against his own *principal?*" Teddy asked.

Chris clutched his knees and rocked back and forth joyfully. "Ain't that *great?* Go on, Gordie!"

I had them now. They were all leaning forward. I felt an intoxicating sense of power. I tossed my empty Coke bottle into the woods and scrunched around a little bit to get comfortable. I remember hearing the chickadee again, off in the woods, farther away now, lifting its monotonous, endless call into the sky: *dee-dee-dee-dee* . . .

"So he gets this idea," I said. "The greatest revenge idea a kid ever had. The big night comes—the end of Pioneer Days. The pie-eating contest comes just before the fireworks. The Main Street of Gretna has been closed off so people can walk around in it, and there's this big platform set up right in the street. There's bunting hanging down and a big crowd in front. There's also a photographer from the paper, to get a picture of the winner with blueberries all over his face, because it turned out to be blueberry pies that year. Also, I almost forgot to tell you this, they had to eat the pies with their hands tied behind their backs. So, dig it, they come up onto the platform . . ."

16

From *The Revenge of Lard Ass Hogan,* by Gordon Lachance. Originally published in *Cavalier* magazine, March, 1975. Used by permission.

They came up onto the platform one by one and stood behind a long trestle table covered with a linen cloth. The table was stacked high with pies and stood at the edge of the platform. Above it were looped necklaces of bare 100-watt bulbs, moths and night-fliers banging softly against them and haloing them. Above the platform, bathed in spotlights, was a long sign which read: THE GREAT GRETNA PIE-EAT OF 1960! To either side of this sign hung battered loudspeakers, supplied by Chuck Day of the Great Day Appliance Shop. Bill Travis, the reigning champion, was Chuck's cousin.

As each contestant came up, his hands bound behind him and his shirtfront open, like Sydney Carton on his way to the guillotine, Mayor Charbonneau would announce his name over Chuck's PA system and tie a large white bib around his neck. Calvin Spier received token applause only; in spite of his belly, which was the size of a twenty-gallon waterbarrel, he was considered an underdog second only to the Hogan kid (most considered Lard Ass a comer, but too young and inexperienced to do much this year).

After Spier, Bob Cormier was introduced. Cormier was a disc jockey who did a popular afternoon program at WLAM in Lewiston. He got a bigger hand, accompanied by a few screams from the teenaged girls in the audience. The girls thought he was "cute." John Wiggins, principal of Gretna Elementary School, followed Cormier. He received a hearty cheer from the older section of the audience—and a few scattered boos from the fractious members of his student body. Wiggins managed to beam paternally and frown sternly down on the audience at the same time.

Next, Mayor Charbonneau introduced Lard Ass.

"A new participant in the annual Great Gretna Pie-Eat, but one we expect great things from in the future . . . *young Master David Hogan!*" Lard Ass got a big round of applause as Mayor Charbonneau tied on his bib, and as it was dying away, a rehearsed Greek chorus just beyond the reach of the 100-watt bulbs cried out in wicked unison: *"Go-get-'em-Lard-Ass!"*

There were muffled shrieks of laughter, running footsteps, a few shadows that no one could (or would) identify, some nervous laughter, some judicial frowns (the largest from Hizzoner Charbonneau, the most visible figure of authority). Lard Ass himself appeared to not even notice. The small smile greasing his thick lips and creasing his thick chops did not change as the Mayor, still frowning largely, tied his bib around his neck and told him not to pay any attention to fools in the audience (as if the Mayor had even the faintest inkling of what monstrous fools Lard Ass Hogan had suffered and would continue to suffer as he rumbled through life like a Nazi Tiger tank). The Mayor's breath was warm and smelled of beer.

The last contestant to mount the bunting-decorated stage drew the loudest and most sustained applause; this was the legendary Bill Travis, six feet five inches tall, gangling, voracious. Travis was a mechanic at the local Amoco station down by the railyard, a likeable fellow if there ever was one.

It was common knowledge around town that there was more involved in the Great Gretna Pie-Eat than a mere five dollars—at least, for Bill Travis there was. There were two reasons for this. First, people always came by the station to congratulate Bill after he won the contest, and most everyone who came to congratulate stayed to get his gas-tank filled. And the two garage-bays were sometimes booked up for a solid month after the contest. Folks would come in to get a muffler replaced or their wheelbearings greased, and would sit in the theater chairs ranged along one wall (Jerry Maling, who owned the Amoco, had salvaged them from the old Gem Theater when it was torn down in 1957), drinking Cokes and Moxies from out of the machine and gassing with Bill about the contest as he changed sparkplugs or rolled around on a crawlie-wheelie under someone's International Harvester pickup, looking for holes in the exhaust system. Bill always seemed willing to talk, which was one of the reasons he was so well-liked in Gretna.

There was some dispute around town as to whether Jerry Maling gave Bill a flat bonus for the extra business his yearly feat (or yearly eat, if you prefer) brought in, or if he got an out-and-out raise. Whatever way it was, there could be no doubt that Travis did much better than most small-town wrench jockeys. He had a nice-looking two-story ranch out on the Sabbatus Road, and certain snide people referred to it as "the house that pies built." That was probably an exaggeration, but Bill had it coming another way—which brings us to the second reason there was more in it for Travis than just five dollars.

The Pie-Eat was a hot wagering event in Gretna. Perhaps most people only came to laugh, but a goodly minority also came to lay their money down. Contestants were observed and discussed by these bettors as ardently as thoroughbreds are observed and discussed by racing touts. The wagerers accosted contestants' friends, relatives, even mere acquaintances. They pried out any and all details concerning the contestants' eating habits. There was always a lot of discussion about that year's official pie—apple was considered a "heavy" pie, apricot a "light" one (although a contestant had to resign himself to a day or two of the trots after downing three or four apricot pies). That year's official pie, blueberry, was considered a happy medium. Bettors, of course, were particularly interested in their man's stomach for blueberry dishes. How did he do on blueberry buckle? Did he favor blueberry jam over strawberry preserves? Had he been known to sprinkle blueberries on his breakfast cereal, or was he strictly a bananas-and-cream sort of fellow?

There were other questions of some moment. Was he a fast eater who slowed down or a slow eater who started to speed up as things got serious or just a good steady all-around trencherman? How many hotdogs could he put away while watching a Babe Ruth League game down at the St. Dom's baseball field? Was he much of a beer-drinker, and, if so, how many bottles did he usually put away in the course of an evening? Was he a belcher? It was believed that a good belcher was a bit tougher to beat over the long haul.

All of this and other information was sifted, the odds laid, the bets made. How much money actually changed hands during the week or so following pie-night I have no way of knowing, but if you held a gun to my head and forced me to guess, I'd put it at close to a thousand dollars— that probably sounds like a pretty paltry figure, but it was a lot of money to be passing around in such a small town fifteen years ago.

And because the contest was honest and a strict time-limit of ten minutes was observed, no one objected to a competitor betting on himself, and Bill Travis did so every year. Talk was, as he nodded, smiling, to his audience on that summer night in 1960, that he had bet a substantial amount on himself again, and that the best he had been able to do this year was one-for-five odds. If you're not the betting type, let me explain it this way: he'd have to put two hundred and fifty dollars at risk to win fifty. Not a good deal at all, but it was the price of success—and as he stood there, soaking up the applause and smiling easy, he didn't look too worried about it.

"And the defending champeen," Mayor Charbonneau trumpeted, "Gretna's own *Bill Travis!*"

"Hoo, Bill!"

"How many you goin through tonight, Bill?"

"You goin for ten, Billy-boy?"

"I got a two-spot on you, Bill! Don't let me down, boy!"

"Save me one of those pies, Trav!"

Nodding and smiling with all proper modesty, Bill Travis allowed the mayor to tie his bib around his neck. Then he sat down at the far right end of the table, near the place where Mayor Charbonneau would stand during the contest. From right to left, then, the eaters were Bill Travis, David "Lard Ass" Hogan, Bob Cormier, principal John Wiggins, and Calvin Spier holding down the stool on the far left.

Mayor Charbonneau introduced Sylvia Dodge, who was even more of a contest figure than Bill Travis himself. She had been President of the Gretna Ladies' Auxiliary for years beyond telling (since the First Manassas, according to some town wits), and it was she who oversaw the baking of each year's pies, strictly subjecting each to her own rigorous quality control, which included a weigh-in ceremony on Mr. Bancichek's butcher's scales down at the Freedom Market—this to make sure that each pie weighed within an ounce of the others.

Sylvia smiled regally down at the crowd, her blue hair twinkling under the hot glow of the lightbulbs. She made a short speech about how glad she was that so much of the town had turned out to celebrate their hardy pioneer forebears, the people who made this country great, for it *was* great, not only on the grassroots level where Mayor Charbonneau would be leading the local Republicans to the hallowed seats of town govern-ment again in November, but on the national level where the team of Nixon and Lodge would take the torch of freedom from Our Great and Beloved General and hold it high for—

Calvin Spier's belly rumbled noisily—*goinnngg!* There was laughter and even some applause. Sylvia Dodge, who knew perfectly well that Calvin was both a Democrat and a Catholic (either would have been for-givable alone, but the two combined, never), managed to blush, smile, and look furious all at the same time. She cleared her throat and wound up with a ringing exhortation to every boy and girl in the audience, tell-ing them to always hold the red, white, and blue high, both in their hands and in their hearts, and to remember that smoking was a dirty, evil habit which made you cough. The boys and girls in the audience, most of whom would be wearing peace medallions and smoking not Camels but marijuana in another eight years, shuffled their feet and waited for the action to begin.

"Less talk, more eatin!" someone in the back row called, and there was another burst of applause—it was heartier this time.

Mayor Charbonneau handed Sylvia a stopwatch and a silver police whistle, which she would blow at the end of the ten minutes of all-out pie-eating. Mayor Charbonneau would then step forward and hold up the hand of the winner.

"Are you *ready*??" Hizzoner's voice rolled triumphantly through the Great Day PA and off down Main Street.

The five pie-eaters declared they were ready.

"Are you *SET*??" Hizzoner enquired further.

The eaters growled that they were indeed set. Down-street, a boy set off a rattling skein of firecrackers.

Mayor Charbonneau raised one pudgy hand and then dropped it. *"GO!!!"*

Five heads dropped into five pie-plates. The sound was like five large feet stamping firmly into mud. Wet chomping noises rose on the mild night air and then were blotted out as the bettors and partisans in the crowd began to cheer on their favorites. And no more than the first pie had been demolished before most people realized that a possible upset was in the making.

Lard Ass Hogan, a seven-to-one underdog because of his age and inexperience, was eating like a boy possessed. His jaws machine-gunned up crust (the contest rules required that only the top crust of the pie be eaten, not the bottom), and when that had disappeared, a huge sucking sound issued from between his lips. It was like the sound of an industrial vacuum cleaner going to work. Then his whole head disappeared into the pie-plate. He raised it fifteen seconds later to indicate he was done. His cheeks and forehead were smeared with blueberry juice, and he looked like an extra in a minstrel show. He was done—done before the legendary Bill Travis had finished *half* of *his* first pie.

Startled applause went up as the Mayor examined Lard Ass's pie-plate and pronounced it clean enough. He whipped a second pie into place before the pace-maker. Lard Ass had gobbled a regulation-size pie in just forty-two seconds. It was a contest record.

He went at the second pie even more furiously yet, his head bobbing and smooching in the soft blueberry filling, and Bill Travis threw him a worried glance as he called for his second blueberry pie. As he told friends later, he felt he was in a real contest for the first time since 1957, when George Gamache gobbled three pies in four minutes and then fainted dead away. He had to wonder, he said, if he was up against a boy or a demon. He thought of the money he had riding on this and redoubled his efforts.

But if Travis had redoubled, Lard Ass had trebled. Blueberries flew from his second pie-dish, staining the tablecloth around him like a Jackson Pollock painting. There were blueberries in his hair, blueberries on

his bib, blueberries standing out on his forehead as if, in an agony of concentration, he had actually begun to *sweat* blueberries.

"Done!" he cried, lifting his head from his second pie-dish before Bill
Travis had even consumed the crust on his new pie.

"Better slow down, boy," Hizzoner murmured. Charbonneau himself
had ten dollars riding on Bill Travis. "You got to pace yourself if you want
to hold out."

It was as if Lard Ass hadn't heard. He tore into his third pie with lunatic
speed, jaws moving with lightning rapidity. And then—

But I must interrupt for a moment to tell you that there was an empty
bottle in the medicine cabinet at Lard Ass Hogan's house. Earlier, that
bottle had been three-quarters full of pearl-yellow castor oil, perhaps
the most noxious fluid that the good Lord, in His Infinite wisdom, ever
allowed upon or beneath the face of the earth. Lard Ass had emptied
the bottle himself, drinking every last drop and then licking the rim, his
mouth twisting, his belly gagging sourly, his brain filled with thoughts of
sweet revenge.

And as he rapidly worked his way through his third pie (Calvin Spier,
dead last as predicted, had not yet finished his first), Lard Ass began to
deliberately torture himself with grisly fantasies. He was not eating pies
at all; he was eating cowflops. He was eating great big gobs of greasy
grimy gopher-guts. He was eating diced-up woodchuck intestines with
blueberry sauce poured over them. *Rancid* blueberry sauce.

He finished his third pie and called for his fourth, now one full pie
ahead of the legendary Bill Travis. The fickle crowd, sensing a new and
unexpected champ in the making, began to cheer him on lustily.

But Lard Ass had no hope or intention of winning. He could not have
continued at the pace he was currently setting if his own mother's life
had been the prize. And besides, winning for him was losing; revenge
was the only blue ribbon he sought. His belly groaning with castor oil, his
throat opening and closing sickly, he finished his fourth pie and called
for his fifth, the Ultimate Pie—Blueberries Become Electra, so to speak.
He dropped his head into the dish, breaking the crust, and snuffled blue-

berries up his nose. Blueberries went down his shirt. The contents of his stomach seemed to suddenly gain weight. He chewed up pasty pastry crust and swallowed it. He inhaled blueberries.

And suddenly the moment of revenge was at hand. His stomach, loaded beyond endurance, revolted. It clenched like a strong hand encased in a slick rubber glove. His throat opened.

Lard Ass raised his head.

He grinned at Bill Travis with blue teeth.

Puke rumbled up his throat like a six-ton Peterbilt shooting through a tunnel.

It roared out of his mouth in huge blue-and-yellow glurt, warm and gaily steaming. It covered Bill Travis, who only had time to utter one nonsense syllable—*"Goog!"* was what it sounded like. Women in the audience screamed. Calvin Spier, who had watched this unannounced event with a numb and surprised expression on his face, leaned conversationally over the table as if to explain to the gaping audience just what was happening, and puked on the head of Marguerite Charbonneau, the Mayor's wife. She screamed and backed away, pawing futilely at her hair, which was now covered with a mixture of crushed berries, baked beans, and partially digested frankfurters (the latter two had been Cal Spier's dinner). She turned to her good friend Maria Lavin and threw up on the front of Maria's buckskin jacket.

In rapid succession, like a replay of the firecrackers:

Bill Travis blew a great—and seemingly supercharged—jet of vomit out over the first two rows of spectators, his stunned face proclaiming to one and all, *Man, I just can't believe I'm doing this;*

Chuck Day, who had received a generous portion of Bill Travis's surprise gift, threw up on his Hush Puppies and then blinked at them wonderingly, knowing full well that stuff would *never* come off suede;

John Wiggins, principal of Gretna Elementary, opened his bluelined mouth and said reprovingly: "Really, this has . . . *YURRK!"* As befitted a man of his breeding and position, he did it in his own pie-plate;

Hizzoner Charbonneau, who found himself suddenly presiding over what must have seemed more like a stomach-flu hospital ward than a pie-eating contest, opened his mouth to call the whole thing off and upchucked all over the microphone.

"Jesus save us!" moaned Sylvia Dodge, and then her outraged supper—fried clams, cole slaw, butter-and-sugar corn (two ears' worth), and a generous helping of Muriel Harrington's Bosco chocolate cake—bolted out the emergency exit and landed with a large wet splash on the back of the Mayor's Robert Hall suitcoat.

Lard Ass Hogan, now at the absolute apogee of his young life, beamed happily out over the audience. Puke was everywhere. People staggered around in drunken circles, holding their throats and making weak cawing noises. Somebody's pet Pekingese ran past the stage, yapping crazily, and a man wearing jeans and a Western-style silk shirt threw up on it, nearly drowning it. Mrs. Brockway, the Methodist minister's wife, made a long, basso belching noise which was followed by a gusher of degenerated roast beef and mashed potatoes and apple cobbler. The cobbler looked as if it might have been good when it first went down. Jerry Maling, who had come to see his pet mechanic walk away with all the marbles again, decided to get the righteous fuck out of this madhouse. He got about fifteen yards before tripping over a kid's little red wagon and realizing he had landed in a puddle of warm bile. Jerry tossed his cookies in his own lap and told folks later he only thanked Providence he had been wearing his coveralls. And Miss Norman, who taught Latin and English Fundamentals at the Gretna Consolidated High School, vomited into her own purse in an agony of propriety.

Lard Ass Hogan watched it all, his large face calm and beaming, his stomach suddenly sweet and steady with a warm balm it might never know again—that balm was a feeling of utter and complete satisfaction. He stood up, took the slightly tacky microphone from the trembling hand of Mayor Charbonneau, and said . . .

17

" 'I declare this contest a draw.' Then he puts the mike down, walks off the back of the platform, and goes straight home. His mother's there, on account of she couldn't get a babysitter for Lard Ass's little sister, who was only two. And as soon as he comes in, all covered with puke and pie-drool, still wearing his bib, she says, 'Davie, did you win?' But he doesn't say a fuckin word, you know. Just goes upstairs to his room, locks the door, and lays down on his bed."

I downed the last swallow in Chris's Coke and tossed it into the woods.

"Yeah, that's cool, then what happened?" Teddy asked eagerly.

"I don't know."

"What do you mean, you don't *know*?" Teddy asked.

"It means it's the end. When you don't know what happens next, that's the end."

"*Whaaaat?*" Vern cried. There was an upset, suspicious look on his face, like he thought maybe he'd just gotten rooked playing penny-up Bingo at the Topsham Fair. "What's all this happy crappy? How'd it come *out!*"

"You have to use your imagination," Chris said patiently.

"No, I ain't!" Vern said angrily. "*He's* supposed to use *his* imagination! He made up the fuckin story!"

"Yeah, what happened to the cat?" Teddy persisted. "Come on, Gordie, tell us."

"I think his dad was at the Pie-Eat and when he came home he beat the living crap out of Lard Ass."

"Yeah, right," Chris said. "I bet that's just what happened."

"And," I said, "the kids went right on calling him Lard Ass. Except that maybe some of them started calling him Puke-Yer-Guts, too."

"That ending sucks," Teddy said sadly.

"That's why I didn't want to tell it."

"You could have made it so he shot his father and ran away and joined the Texas Rangers," Teddy said. "How about that?"

Chris and I exchanged a glance. Chris raised one shoulder in a barely perceptible shrug.

"I guess so," I said.

"Hey, you got any new Le Dio stories, Gordie?"

"Not just now. Maybe I'll think of some." I didn't want to upset Teddy, but I wasn't very interested in checking out what was happening in Le Dio, either. "Sorry you didn't go for this one better."

"Nah, it was good," Teddy said. "Right up to the end, it was good. All that pukin was really cool."

"Yeah, that was cool, really gross," Vern agreed. "But Teddy's right about the ending. It was sort of a gyp."

"Yeah," I said, and sighed.

Chris stood up. "Let's do some walking," he said. It was still bright daylight, the sky a hot, steely blue, but our shadows had begun to trail out long. I remember that as a kid, September days always seemed to end much too soon, catching me by surprise—it was as if something inside my heart expected it to always be June, with daylight lingering in the sky until almost nine-thirty. "What time is it, Gordie?"

I looked at my watch and was astonished to see it was after five.

"Yeah, let's go," Teddy said. "But let's make camp before dark so we can see to get wood and stuff. I'm getting hungry, too."

"Six-thirty," Chris promised. "Okay with you guys?"

It was. We started to walk again, using the cinders beside the tracks now. Soon the river was so far behind us we couldn't even hear its sound. Mosquitoes hummed and I slapped one off my neck. Vern and Teddy were walking up ahead, working out some sort of complicated comic-book trade. Chris was beside me, hands in his pockets, shirt slapping against his knees and thighs like an apron.

"I got some Winstons," he said. "Hawked em off my old man's dresser. One apiece. For after supper."

"Yeah? That's boss."

"That's when a cigarette tastes best," Chris said. "After supper."

"Right."

We walked in silence for awhile.

"That's a really fine story," Chris said suddenly. "They're just a little too dumb to understand."

"No, it's not that hot. It's a mumbler."

"That's what you always say. Don't give me that bullshit you don't believe. Are you gonna write it down? The story?"

"Probably. But not for awhile. I can't write em down right after I tell em. It'll keep."

"What Vern said? About the ending being a gyp?"

"Yeah?"

Chris laughed. "*Life's* a gyp, you know it? I mean, look at us."

"Nah, we have a great time."

"Sure," Chris said. "All the fuckin time, you wet."

I laughed. Chris did, too.

"They come outta you just like bubbles out of soda-pop," he said after awhile.

"What does?" But I thought I knew what he meant.

"The stories. That really bugs me, man. It's like you could tell a million stories and still only get the ones on top. You'll be a great writer someday, Gordie."

"No, I don't think so."

"Yeah, you will. Maybe you'll even write about us guys if you ever get hard up for material."

"Have to be pretty fuckin hard up." I gave him the elbow.

There was another period of silence and then he asked suddenly: "You ready for school?"

I shrugged. Who ever was? You got a little excited thinking about going back, seeing your friends; you were curious about your new teachers and what they would be like—pretty young things just out of teachers' college that you could rag or some old topkick that had been there since the Alamo. In a funny way you could even get excited about the long droning classes, because as the summer vacation neared its end you sometimes got bored enough to believe you could learn something. But summer boredom was nothing like the school boredom that always set in by the end of the second week, and by the beginning of the third week you got down to the *real* business: Could you hit Stinky Fiske in the back of the head with your Art-Gum while the teacher was putting The Principal Exports of South America on the board? How many good loud squeaks could you get off on the varnished surface of your desk if your hands were real sweaty? Who could cut the loudest farts in the locker room while changing up for phys ed? How many girls could you get to play Who Goosed the Moose during lunch hour? Higher learning, baby.

"Junior High," Chris said. "And you know what, Gordie? By next June, we'll all be quits."

"What are you talking about? Why would *that* happen?"

"It's not gonna be like grammar school, that's why. You'll be in the college courses. Me and Teddy and Vern, we'll all be in the shop courses, playing pocket-pool with the rest of the retards, making ashtrays and birdhouses. Vern might even have to go into Remedial. You'll meet a lot of new guys. Smart guys. That's just the way it works, Gordie. That's how they got it set up."

"Meet a lot of pussies is what you mean," I said.

He gripped my arm. "No, man. Don't say that. Don't even *think* that. They'll get your stories. Not like Vern and Teddy."

"Fuck the stories. I'm not going in with a lot of pussies. No sir."

"If you don't, then you're an asshole."

"What's asshole about wanting to be with your friends?"

He looked at me thoughtfully, as if deciding whether or not to tell me something. We had slowed down: Vern and Teddy had pulled almost half a mile ahead. The sun, lower now, came at us through the overlacing trees in broken, dusty shafts, turning everything gold—but it was a tawdry gold, dime-store gold, if you can dig that. The tracks stretched ahead of us in the gloom that was just starting to gather— they seemed almost to twinkle. Star-pricks of light stood out on them here and there, as if some nutty rich guy masquerading as a common laborer had decided to embed a diamond in the steel every sixty yards or so. It was still hot. The sweat rolled off us, slicking our bodies.

"It's asshole if your friends can drag you down," Chris said finally. "I know about you and your folks. They don't give a shit about you. Your big brother was the one they cared about. Like my dad, when Frank got thrown into the stockade in Portsmouth. That was when he started always bein mad at us other kids and hitting us all the time. Your dad doesn't beat on you, but maybe that's even worse. He's got you asleep. You could tell him you were enrolling in the fuckin shop division and you know what he'd do? He'd turn to the next page in his paper and say: Well, that's nice, Gordon, go ask your mother what's for dinner. And don't try to tell me different. I've met him."

I didn't try to tell him different. It's scary to find out that someone else, even a friend, knows just how things are with you.

"You're just a kid, Gordie—"

"Gee, thanks, Dad."

"I wish to fuck I *was* your father!" he said angrily. "You wouldn't go around talking about takin those stupid shop courses if I was! It's like God gave you something, all those stories you can make up, and He said: This is what we got for you, kid. Try not to lose it. But kids lose *everything* unless somebody looks out for them and if your folks are too fucked up to do it then maybe I ought to."

His face looked like he was expecting me to take a swing at him; it was set and unhappy in the green-gold late afternoon light. He had broken the cardinal rule for kids in those days. You could say anything about another kid, you could rank him to the dogs and back, but you didn't say a bad word *ever* about his mom and dad. That was the Fabled Automatic, the same way not inviting your Catholic friends home to dinner on Friday unless you'd checked first to make sure you weren't having meat was the Fabled Automatic. If a kid ranked out your mom and dad, you had to feed him some knuckles.

"Those stories you tell, they're no good to anybody but you, Gordie. If you go along with us just because you don't want the gang to break up, you'll wind up just another grunt, makin C's to get on the teams. You'll get to High and take the same fuckin shop courses and throw erasers and pull your meat along with the rest of the grunts. Get detentions. Fuckin *suspensions*. And after awhile all you'll care about is gettin a car so you can take some skag to the hops or down to the fuckin Twin Bridges Tavern. Then you'll knock her up and spend the rest of your life in the mill or some fuckin shoeshop in Auburn or maybe even up to Hillcrest pluckin chickens. And that pie story will never get written down. *Nothin'*ll get written down. Cause you'll just be another wiseguy with shit for brains."

Chris Chambers was twelve when he said all that to me. But while he was saying it his face crumpled and folded into something older, oldest, ageless. He spoke tonelessly, colorlessly, but nevertheless, what he said struck terror into my bowels. It was as if he had lived that whole life already, that life where they tell you to step right up and spin the Wheel of Fortune, and it spins so pretty and the guy steps on a pedal and it comes up double zeros, house number, everybody loses. They give you a free pass and then they turn on the rain machine, pretty funny, huh, a joke even Vern Tessio could appreciate.

He grabbed my naked arm and his fingers closed tight. They dug grooves in my flesh. They ground at the bones. His eyes were hooded and dead—so dead, man, that he might have just fallen out of his own coffin.

"I know what people think of my family in this town. I know what they think of me and what they expect. Nobody even *asked* me if I took the milk-money that time. I just got a three-day vacation."

"*Did* you take it?" I asked. I had never asked him before, and if you had told me I ever would, I would have called you crazy. The words came out in a little dry bullet.

"Yeah," he said. "Yeah, I took it." He was silent for a moment, looking ahead at Teddy and Vern. "You knew I took it, Teddy knew. *Everybody* knew. Even Vern knew, I think."

I started to deny it, and then closed my mouth. He was right. No matter what I might have said to my mother and father about how a person was supposed to be innocent until proved guilty, I had known.

"Then maybe I was sorry and tried to give it back," Chris said.

I stared at him, my eyes widening. "You tried to give it *back?*"

"*Maybe,* I said. Just *maybe.* And maybe I took it to old lady Simons and told her, and maybe the money was all there but I got a three-day vacation *anyway,* because the money never showed up. And maybe the next week old lady Simons had this brand-new skirt on when she came to school."

I stared at Chris, speechless with horror. He smiled at me, but it was a crimped, terrible smile that never touched his eyes.

"Just *maybe*," he said, but I remembered the new skirt—a light brown paisley, sort of full. I remembered thinking that it made old lady Simons look younger, almost pretty.

"Chris, how much was that milk-money?"

"Almost seven bucks."

"Christ," I whispered.

"So just say that *I* stole the milk-money but then old lady Simons stole it from *me*. Just suppose I told that story. Me, Chris Chambers. Kid brother of Frank Chambers and Eyeball Chambers. You think anybody would have believed it?"

"No way," I whispered. "Jesus Christ!"

He smiled his wintry, awful smile. "And do you think that bitch would have dared try something like that if it had been one of those dootchbags from up on The View that had taken the money?"

"No," I said.

"Yeah, if it had been one of them, Simons would have said: 'Kay, 'kay, we'll forget it this time, but we're gonna spank your wrist real hard and if you ever do it again we'll have to spank *both* wrists. But *me* . . . well, maybe she had her eye on that skirt for a long time. Anyway, she saw her chance and she took it. I was the stupid one for even trying to give that money back. But I never thought . . . I never thought that a *teacher* . . . oh, who gives a fuck, anyway? Why am I even talkin about it?"

He swiped an arm angrily across his eyes and I realized he was almost crying.

"Chris," I said, "why don't you go into the college courses? You're smart enough."

"They decide all of that in the office. And in their smart little conferences. The teachers, they sit around in this big circle-jerk and all they say is Yeah, Yeah, Right, Right. All they give a fuck about is whether you behaved yourself in grammar school and what the town thinks of your family. All they're deciding is whether or not you'll contaminate all those precious college-course dootchbags. But maybe I'll try to work myself up. I don't know if I could do it, but I might try. Because I want to get out of Castle Rock and go to college and never see my old man or any of my brothers again. I want to go someplace where nobody knows me and I don't have any black marks against me before I start. But I don't know if I can do it."

"Why not?"

"People. People drag you down."

"Who?" I asked, thinking he must mean the teachers, or adult monsters like Miss Simons, who had wanted a new skirt, or maybe his brother Eyeball who hung around with Ace and Billy and Charlie and the rest, or maybe his own mom and dad.

But he said: "Your friends drag you down, Gordie. Don't you know that?" He pointed at Vern and Teddy, who were standing and waiting for us to catch up. They were laughing about something; in fact, Vern was just about busting a gut. "Your friends do. They're like drowning guys that are holding onto your legs. You can't save them. You can only drown with them."

"Come on, you fuckin slowpokes!" Vern shouted, still laughing.

"Yeah, comin!" Chris called, and before I could say anything else, he began to run. I ran, too, but he caught up to them before I could catch up to him.

18

We went another mile and then decided to camp for the night. There was still some daylight left, but nobody really wanted to use it. We were pooped from the scene at the dump and from our scare on the train trestle, but it was more than that. We were in Harlow now, in the woods. Somewhere up ahead was a dead kid, probably mangled and covered with flies. Maggots, too, by this time. Nobody wanted to get too close to him with the night coming on. I had read somewhere—in an Algernon Blackwood story, I think—that a guy's ghost hangs out around his dead body until that body is given a decent Christian burial, and there was no way I wanted to wake up in the night and confront the glowing, disembodied ghost of Ray Brower, moaning and gibbering and floating among the dark and rustling pines. By stopping here we figured there had to be at least ten miles between us and him, and of course all four of us knew there were no such things as ghosts, but ten miles seemed just about far enough in case what everybody knew was wrong.

Vern, Chris, and Teddy gathered wood and got a modest little campfire going on a bed of cinders. Chris scraped a bare patch all around the fire—the woods were powder-dry, and he didn't want to take any chances. While they were doing that I sharpened some sticks and made what my brother Denny used to call "Pioneer Drumsticks"—lumps of hamburger pushed onto the ends of green branches. The three of them laughed and bickered over their woodcraft (which was almost nil; there was a Castle Rock Boy Scout troop, but most of the kids who hung around our vacant lot considered it to be an organization made up mostly of pussies), arguing about whether it was better to cook over flames or over coals (a moot point; we were too hungry to wait for coals), whether dried moss would work as kindling, what they would do if they used up all the matches before they got the fire to stay lit. Teddy claimed he could make a fire by rubbing two sticks together. Chris claimed he was so full of shit he squeaked. They didn't have to try; Vern got the small pile of twigs and dry moss to catch from the second match. The day was perfectly still and there was no wind to puff out the light. We all took turns feeding the thin flames until they began to grow stouter on wrist-chunks of wood fetched from an old deadfall some thirty yards into the forest.

When the flames began to die back a little bit, I stuck the sticks holding the Pioneer Drumsticks firmly into the ground at an angle over the fire. We sat around watching them as they shimmered and dripped and finally began to brown. Our stomachs made pre-dinner conversation.

Unable to wait until they were really cooked, we each took one of them, stuck it in a roll, and yanked the hot stick out of the center. They were charred outside, raw inside, and totally delicious. We wolfed them down and wiped the grease from our mouths with our bare arms. Chris opened his pack and took out a tin Band-Aids box (the pistol was way at the bottom of his pack, and because he hadn't told Vern and Teddy, I guessed it was to be our secret). He opened it and gave each of us a battered Winston. We lit them with flaming twigs from the fire and then leaned back, men of the world, watching the cigarette smoke drift away into the soft twilight. None of us inhaled because we might cough and that would mean a day or two of ragging from the others. And it was pleasant enough just to drag and blow, hawking into the fire to hear the sizzle (that was the summer I learned how you can pick out someone who is just learning to smoke: if you're new at it you spit a lot). We were feeling good. We smoked the Winstons down to the filters, then tossed them into the fire.

"Nothin like a smoke after a meal," Teddy said.

"Fucking-A," Vern agreed.

Crickets had started to hum in the green gloom. I looked up at the lane of sky visible through the railroad cut and saw that the blue was now bruising toward purple. Seeing that outrider of twilight made me feel sad and calm at the same time, brave but not really brave, comfortably lonely.

We tromped down a flat place in the underbrush beside the embankment and laid out our bedrolls. Then, for an hour or so, we fed the fire and talked, the kind of talk you can never quite remember once you get past fifteen and discover girls. We talked about who was the best dragger in Castle Rock, if Boston could maybe stay out of the cellar this year, and about the summer just past. Teddy told about the time he had been at White's Beach in Brunswick and some kid had hit his head while diving off the float and almost drowned. We discussed at some length the relative merits of the teachers we had had. We agreed that Mr. Brooks was the biggest pussy in Castle Rock Elementary—he would just about cry if you sassed him back. On the other hand, there was Mrs. Cote (pronounced Cody)—she was just about the meanest bitch God had ever set down on the earth. Vern said he'd heard she hit a kid so hard two years ago that the kid almost went blind. I looked at Chris, wondering if he would say anything about Miss Simons, but he didn't say anything at all, and he didn't see me looking at him—he was looking at Vern and nodding soberly at Vern's story.

We didn't talk about Ray Brower as the dark drew down, but I was thinking about him. There's something horrible and fascinating about the way dark comes to the woods, its coming unsoftened by headlights or streetlights or houselights or neon. It comes with no mothers' voices, calling for their kids to leave off and come on in now, to herald it. If you're used to the town, the coming of the dark in the woods seems more like a natural disaster than a natural phenomenon; it rises like the Castle River rises in the spring.

And as I thought about the body of Ray Brower in this light—or lack of it—what I felt was not queasiness or fear that he would suddenly appear before us, a green and gibbering banshee whose purpose was to drive us back the way we had come before we could disturb his—*its*—peace, but a sudden

115

and unexpected wash of pity that he should be so alone and so defenseless in the dark that was now coming over our side of the earth. If something wanted to eat on him, it would. His mother wasn't here to stop that from happening, and neither was his father, nor Jesus Christ in the company of all the saints. He was dead and he was all alone, flung off the railroad tracks and into the ditch, and I realized that if I didn't stop thinking about it I was going to cry.

So I told a Le Dio story, made up on the spot and not very good, and when it ended as most of my Le Dio stories did, with one lone American dogface coughing out a dying declaration of patriotism and love for the girl back home into the sad and wise face of the platoon sergeant, it was not the white, scared face of some pfc from Castle Rock or White River Junction I saw in my mind's eye but the face of a much younger boy, already dead, his eyes closed, his features troubled, a rill of blood running from the left corner of his mouth to his jawline. And in back of him, instead of the shattered shops and churches of my Le Dio dreamscape, I saw only dark forest and the cindered railway bed bulking against the starry sky like a prehistoric burial mound.

19

I came awake in the middle of the night, disoriented, wondering why it was so chilly in my bedroom and who had left the windows open. Denny, maybe. I had been dreaming of Denny, something about body-surfing at Harrison State Park. But it had been four years ago that we had done that.

This wasn't my room; this was someplace else. Somebody was holding me in a mighty bearhug, somebody else was pressed against my back, and a shadowy third was crouched beside me, head cocked in a listening attitude.

"What the fuck?" I asked in honest puzzlement.

A long-drawn-out groan in answer. It sounded like Vern.

That brought things into focus, and I remembered where I was . . . but what was everybody doing awake in the middle of the night? Or had I only been asleep for seconds? No, that couldn't be, because a thin sliver of moon was floating dead center in an inky sky.

"Don't let it get me!" Vern gibbered. "I swear I'll be a good boy, I won't do nothin bad, I'll put the ring up before I take a piss, I'll . . . I'll . . ." With some astonishment I realized that I was listening to a prayer—or at least the Vern Tessio equivalent of a prayer.

I sat bolt upright, scared. "Chris?"

"Shut up, Vern," Chris said. He was the one crouching and listening. "It's nothing."

"Oh, yes it is," Teddy said ominously. "It's something."

"*What* is?" I asked. I was still sleepy and disoriented, unstrung from my place in space and time. It scared me that I had come in late on whatever had developed—too late to defend myself properly, maybe.

Then, as if to answer my question, a long and hollow scream rose languidly from the woods—it was the sort of scream you might expect from a woman dying in extreme agony and extreme fear.

"Oh-dear-to-Jesus!" Vern whimpered, his voice high and filled with tears. He re-applied the bearhug that had awakened me, making it hard for me to breathe and adding to my own terror. I threw him loose with an effort but he scrambled right back beside me like a puppy which can't think of anyplace else to go.

"It's that Brower kid," Teddy whispered hoarsely. "His ghost's out walkin in the woods."

"Oh God!" Vern screamed, apparently not crazy about that

idea at all. "I promise I won't hawk no more dirty books out of Dahlie's Market! I promise I won't give my carrots to the dog no more! I . . . I . . . I . . ." He floundered there, wanting to bribe God with everything but unable to think of anything really good in the extremity of his fear. *"I won't smoke no more unfiltered cigarettes! I won't say no bad swears! I won't put my Bazooka in the offerin plate! I won't—"*

"Shut up, Vern," Chris said, and beneath his usual authoritative toughness I could hear the hollow boom of awe. I wondered if his arms and back and belly were as stiff with gooseflesh as my own were, and if the hair on the nape of his neck was trying to stand up in hackles, as mine was.

Vern's voice dropped to a whisper as he continued to expand the reforms he planned to institute if God would only let him live through this night.

"It's a bird, isn't it?" I asked Chris.

"No. At least, I don't think so. I think it's a wildcat. My dad says they scream bloody murder when they're getting ready to mate. Sounds like a woman, doesn't it?"

"Yeah," I said. My voice hitched in the middle of the word and two ice-cubes broke off in the gap.

"But no woman could scream that loud," Chris said . . . and then added helplessly: "Could she, Gordie?"

"It's his ghost," Teddy whispered again. His eyeglasses reflected the moonlight in weak, somehow dreamy smears. "I'm gonna go look for it."

I don't think he was serious, but we took no chances. When he started to get up, Chris and I hauled him back down. Perhaps we were too rough with him, but our muscles had been turned to cables with fear.

"Let me up, fuckheads!" Teddy hissed, struggling. "If I say I wanna go look for it, then I'm gonna go look for it! I wanna see it! I wanna see the ghost! I wanna see if—"

The wild, sobbing cry rose into the night again, cutting the air like a knife with a crystal blade, freezing us with our hands on Teddy—if he'd been a flag, we would have looked like that picture of the Marines claiming Iwo Jima. The scream climbed with a crazy ease through octave after octave, finally reaching a glassy, freezing edge. It hung there for a moment and then whirled back down again, disappearing into an impossible bass register that buzzed like a monstrous honeybee. This was followed by a burst of what sounded like mad laughter . . . and then there was silence again.

"Jesus H Baldheaded Christ," Teddy whispered, and he talked no more of going into the woods to see what was making that screaming noise. All four of us huddled up together and I thought of running. I doubt if I was the only one. If we had been tenting in Vern's field—where our folks *thought* we were—we probably *would* have run. But Castle Rock was too far, and the thought of trying to run across that trestle in the dark made my blood freeze. Running deeper into Harlow and closer to the corpse of Ray Brower was equally unthinkable. We were stuck. If there was a ha'ant out there in the woods—what my dad called a Goosalum—and it wanted us, it would probably get us.

Chris proposed we keep a guard and everyone was agreeable to that. We flipped for watches and Vern got the first one. I got the last. Vern sat up cross-legged by the husk of the campfire while the rest of us lay down again. We huddled together like sheep.

I was positive that sleep would be impossible, but I did sleep—a light, uneasy sleep that skimmed through unconsciousness like a sub with its periscope up. My half-sleeping dreams were populated with wild cries that might have been real or might have only been products of my imagination. I saw—or thought I saw—something white and shapeless steal through the trees like a grotesquely ambulatory bedsheet.

At last I slipped into something I knew was a dream. Chris and I were swimming at White's Beach, a gravel-pit in Brunswick that had been turned into a miniature lake when the gravel-diggers struck water. It was where Teddy had seen the kid hit his head and almost drown.

In my dream we were out over our heads, stroking lazily along, with a hot July sun blazing down. From behind us, on the float, came cries and shouts and yells of laughter as kids climbed and dived or climbed and were pushed. I could hear the empty kerosene drums that held the float up clanging and booming together—a sound not unlike that of churchbells, which are so solemn and emptily profound. On the sand-and-gravel beach, oiled bodies lay face down on blankets, little kids with buckets squatted on the verge of the water or sat happily flipping muck into their hair with plastic shovels, and teenagers clustered in grinning groups, watching the young girls promenade endlessly back and forth in pairs and trios, never alone, the secret places of their bodies wrapped in Jantzen tank suits. People walked up the hot sand on the balls of their feet, wincing, to the snackbar. They came back with chips, Devil Dogs, Red Ball Popsicles.

Mrs. Cote drifted past us on an inflatable rubber raft. She was lying on her back, dressed in her typical September-to-June school uniform: a gray two-piece suit with a thick sweater instead of a blouse under the jacket, a flower pinned over one almost nonexistent breast, thick support hose the color of Canada Mints on her legs. Her black old lady's high-heeled shoes were trailing in the water, making small V's. Her hair was blue-rinsed, like my mother's, and done up in those tight, medicinal-smelling clockspring curls. Her glasses flashed brutally in the sun.

"Watch your steps, boys," she said. "Watch your steps or I'll hit you hard enough to strike you blind. I can do that; I have been given that power by the school board. Now, Mr. Chambers, 'Mending Wall,' if you please. By rote."

"I tried to give the money back," Chris said. "Old lady Simons said okay, but she *took* it! Do you hear me? She *took* it! Now what are you going to do about it? Are you going to whack *her* blind?"

" 'Mending Wall,' Mr. Chambers, if you please. By *rote.*"

Chris threw me a despairing glance, as if to say *Didn't I tell you it would be this way?*, and then began to tread water. He began: " 'Something there is that doesn't love a wall, that sends the frozen-ground-swell under it—' " And then his head went under, his reciting mouth filling with water.

He popped back up, crying: "Help me, Gordie! Help me!"

Then he was dragged under again. Looking into the clear water I could see two bloated, naked corpses holding his ankles. One was Vern and the other was Teddy, and their open eyes were as blank and pupilless as the eyes of Greek statues. Their small pre-pubescent penises floated limply up from their distended bellies like albino strands of kelp. Chris's head broke water again. He held one hand up limply to me and voiced a screaming, womanish cry that rose and rose, ululating in the hot sunny summer air. I looked wildly toward the beach but nobody had heard. The lifeguard, his bronzed, athletic body lolling attractively on the seat at the top of his whitewashed cruciform wooden tower, just went on smiling down at a girl in a red bathing suit. Chris's scream turned into a bubbling water-choked gurgle as the corpses pulled him under again. And as they dragged him down to black water I could see his rippling, distorted eyes turned up to me in a pleading agony; I could see his white starfish hands held helplessly up to the sun-burnished roof of the water. But instead of diving down and trying to save him, I stroked madly for the shore, or at least to a place where the water would not be over my head.

Before I could get there—before I could even get close—I felt a soft, rotted, implacable hand wrap itself around my calf and begin to pull. A scream built up in my chest . . . but before I could utter it, the dream washed away into a grainy facsimile of reality. It was Teddy with his hand on my leg. He was shaking me awake. It was my watch.

Still half in the dream, almost talking in my sleep, I asked him thickly: "You alive, Teddy?"

"No. I'm dead and you're a black nigger," he said crossly. It dispelled the last of the dream. I sat up by the campfire and Teddy lay down.

20

The others slept heavily through the rest of the night. I was in and out, dozing, waking, dozing again. The night was far from silent; I heard the triumphant screech-squawk of a pouncing owl, the tiny cry of some small animal perhaps about to be eaten, a larger something blundering wildly through the undergrowth. Under all of this, a steady tone, were the crickets. There were no more screams. I dozed and woke, woke and dozed, and I suppose if I had been discovered standing such a slipshod watch in Le Dio, I probably would have been courtmartialed and shot.

I snapped more solidly out of my last doze and became aware that something was different. It took me a moment or two to figure it out: although the moon was down, I could see my hands resting on my jeans. My watch said quarter to five. It was dawn.

I stood, hearing my spine crackle, walked two dozen feet away from the limped-together bodies of my friends, and pissed into a clump of sumac. I was starting to shake the night-willies; I could feel them sliding away. It was a fine feeling.

I scrambled up the cinders to the railroad tracks and sat on one of the rails, idly chucking cinders between my feet, in no hurry to wake the others. At that precise moment the new day felt too good to share.

Morning came on apace. The noise of the crickets began to drop, and the shadows under the trees and bushes evaporated like puddles after a shower. The air had that peculiar lack of taste that presages the latest hot day in a famous series of hot days. Birds that had maybe cowered all night just as we had done now began to twitter self-importantly. A wren landed on top of the deadfall from which we had taken our firewood, preened itself, and then flew off.

I don't know how long I sat there on the rail, watching the purple steal out of the sky as noiselessly as it had stolen in the evening before. Long enough for my butt to start complaining anyway. I was about to get up when I looked to my right and saw a deer standing in the railroad bed not ten yards from me.

My heart went up into my throat so high that I think I could have put my hand in my mouth and touched it. My stomach and genitals filled with a hot dry excitement. I didn't move. I couldn't have moved if I had wanted to. Her eyes weren't brown but a dark, dusty black—the kind of velvet you see backgrounding jewelry displays. Her small ears were scuffed suede. She looked serenely at me, head slightly lowered in what I took for curiosity, seeing a kid with his hair in a sleep-scarecrow of whirls and many-tined cowlicks, wearing jeans with cuffs and a brown khaki shirt with the elbows mended and the collar turned up in the hoody tradition of the day. What I was seeing was some sort of gift, something given with a carelessness that was appalling.

We looked at each other for a long time . . . I *think* it was a long time. Then she turned and walked off to the other side of the tracks, white bobtail flipping insouciantly. She found grass and began to crop. I couldn't believe it. She had begun to *crop*. She didn't look back at me and didn't need to; I was frozen solid.

Then the rail started to thrum under my ass and bare seconds later the doe's head came up, cocked back toward Castle Rock. She stood there, her branch-black nose working on the air, coaxing it a little. Then she was gone in three gangling leaps, vanishing into the woods with no sound but one rotted branch, which broke with a sound like a track ref's starter-gun.

I sat there, looking mesmerized at the spot where she had been, until the actual sound of the freight came up through the stillness. Then I skidded back down the bank to where the others were sleeping.

The freight's slow, loud passage woke them up, yawning and scratching. There was some funny, nervous talk about "the case of the screaming ghost," as Chris called it, but not as much as you might imagine. In daylight it seemed more foolish than interesting—almost embarrassing. Best forgotten.

It was on the tip of my tongue to tell them about the deer, but I ended up not doing it. That was one thing I kept to myself. I've never spoken or written of it until just now, today. And I have to tell you that it seems a lesser thing written down, damn near inconsequential. But for me it was the best part of that trip, the cleanest part, and it was a moment I found myself returning to, almost helplessly, when there was trouble in my life—my first day in the bush in Vietnam, and this fellow walked into the clearing where we were with his hand over his nose and when he took his hand away there was no nose there because it had been shot off; the time the doctor told us our youngest son might be hydrocephalic (he turned out just to have an oversized head, thank God); the long, crazy weeks before my mother died. I would find my thoughts turning back to that morning, the scuffed suede of her ears, the white flash of her tail. But eight hundred million Red Chinese don't give a shit, right? The most important things are the hardest to say, because words diminish them. It's hard to make strangers care about the good things in your life.

21

The tracks now bent southwest and ran through tangles of second-growth fir and heavy underbrush. We got a breakfast of late blackberries from some of these bushes, but berries never fill you up; your stomach just gives them a thirty-minute option and then begins growling again. We went back to the tracks—it was about eight o'clock by then—and took five. Our mouths were a dark purple and our naked torsos were scratched from the blackberry brambles. Vern wished glumly aloud for a couple of fried eggs with bacon on the side.

That was the last day of the heat, and I think it was the worst of all. The early scud of clouds melted away and by nine o'clock the sky was a pale steel color that made you feel hotter just looking at it. The sweat rolled and ran from our chests and backs, leaving clean streaks through the accumu-lated soot and grime. Mosquitoes and blackflies whirled and dipped around our heads in aggravating clouds. Knowing that we had long miles to go didn't make us feel any better. Yet the fascination of the thing drew us on and kept us walking faster than we had any business doing, in that heat. We were all crazy to see that kid's body—I can't put it any more simply or honestly than that. Whether it was harmless or whether it turned out to have the power to murder sleep with a hundred mangled dreams, we wanted to see it. I think that we had come to believe we *deserved* to see it.

It was about nine-thirty when Teddy and Chris spotted

water up ahead—they shouted to Vern and me. We ran over to where they were standing. Chris was laughing, delighted. "Look there! Beavers did that!" He pointed.

It was the work of beavers, all right. A large-bore culvert ran under the railroad embankment a little way ahead, and the beavers had sealed the right end with one of their neat and industrious little dams—sticks and branches cemented together with leaves, twigs, and dried mud. Beavers are busy little fuckers, all right. Behind the dam was a clear and shining pool of water, brilliantly mirroring the sunlight. Beaver houses humped up and out of the water in several places—they looked like wooden igloos. A small creek trickled into the far end of the pool, and the trees which bordered it were gnawed a clean bone-white to a height of almost three feet in places.

"Railroad'll clean this shit out pretty soon," Chris said.

"Why?" Vern asked.

"They can't have a pool here," Chris said. "It'd undercut their precious railroad line. That's why they put that culvert in there to start with. They'll shoot them some beavers and scare off the rest and then knock out their dam. Then this'll go back to being a bog, like it probably was before."

"I think that eats the meat," Teddy said.

Chris shrugged. "Who cares about beavers? Not the Great Southern and Western Maine, that's for sure."

"You think it's deep enough to swim in?" Vern asked, looking hungrily at the water.

"One way to find out," Teddy said.

"Who goes first?" I asked.

"Me!" Chris said. He went running down the bank, kicking off his sneakers and untying his shirt from around his waist with a jerk. He pushed his pants and undershorts down with a single shove of his thumbs. He balanced, first on one leg and then on the other, to get his socks. Then he made a shallow dive. He came up shaking his head to get his wet hair out of his eyes. "It's fuckin *great!*" he shouted.

"How deep?" Teddy called back. He had never learned to swim.

Chris stood up in the water and his shoulders broke the surface. I saw something on one of them—a blackish-grayish something. I decided it was a piece of mud and dismissed it. If I had looked more closely I could have saved myself a lot of nightmares later on. "Come on in, you chickens!"

He turned and thrashed off across the pool in a clumsy breast-stroke, turned over, and thrashed back. By then we were all getting undressed. Vern was in next, then me.

Hitting the water was fantastic—clean and cool. I swam across to Chris, loving the silky feel of having nothing on but water. I stood up and we grinned into each other's faces.

"Boss!" We said it at exactly the same instant.

"Fuckin jerkoff," he said, splashed water in my face, and swam off the other way.

We goofed off in the water for almost half an hour before we realized that the pond was full of bloodsuckers. We dived, swam under water, ducked each other. We never knew a thing. Then Vern swam into the shallower part, went under, and stood on his hands. When his legs broke water in a shaky but triumphant V, I saw that they were covered with blackish-gray lumps, just like the one I had seen on Chris's shoulder. They were slugs—big ones.

Chris's mouth dropped open, and I felt all the blood in my body go as cold as dry ice. Teddy screamed, his face going pale. Then all three of us were thrashing for the bank, going just as fast as we could. I know more about freshwater slugs now than I did then, but the fact that they are mostly harmless has done nothing to allay the almost insane horror of them I've had ever since that day in the beaver-pool. They carry a local anesthetic and an anti-coagulant in their alien saliva, which means that the host never feels a thing when they attach themselves. If you don't happen to see them they'll go on feeding until their swelled, loathsome bodies fall off you, sated, or until they actually burst.

We pulled ourselves up on the bank and Teddy went into a hysterical paroxysm as he looked down at himself. He was screaming as he picked the leeches off his naked body.

Vern broke the water and looked at us, puzzled. "What the hell's wrong with h—"

"*Leeches!*" Teddy screamed, pulling two of them off his trembling thighs and throwing them just as far as he could. "Dirty mother-fuckin *bloodsuckers!*" His voice broke shrilly on the last word.

"*OhGodOhGodOhGod!*" Vern cried. He paddled across the pool and stumbled out.

I was still cold; the heat of the day had been suspended. I kept telling myself to catch hold. Not to get screaming. Not to be a pussy. I picked half a dozen off my arms and several more off my chest.

Chris turned his back to me. "Gordie? Are there any more? Take em off if there are, please, Gordie!" There *were* more, five or six, running down his back like grotesque black buttons. I pulled their soft, boneless bodies off him.

I brushed even more off my legs, then got Chris to do my back.

I was starting to relax a little—and that was when I looked down at myself and saw the granddaddy of them all clinging to my testicles, its body swelled to four times its normal size. Its blackish-gray skin had gone a bruised purplish-red. That was when I began to lose control. Not outside, at least not in any big way, but inside, where it counts.

I brushed its slick, glutinous body with the back of my hand.

It held on. I tried to do it again and couldn't bring myself to actually touch it. I turned to Chris, tried to speak, couldn't. I pointed instead. His cheeks, already ashy, went whiter still.

"I can't get it off," I said through numb lips. "You . . . can you . . ."

But he backed away, shaking his head, his mouth twisted. "I can't, Gordie," he said, unable to take his eyes away. "I'm sorry but I can't. No. Oh. No." He turned away, bowed with one hand pressed to his midsection like the butler in a musical comedy, and was sick in a stand of juniper bushes.

You got to hold onto yourself, I thought, looking at the leech that hung off me like a crazy beard. Its body was still visibly swelling. *You got to hold onto yourself and get him. Be tough. It's the last one. The. Last. One.*

I reached down again and picked it off and it burst between my fingers. My own blood ran across my palm and inner wrist in a warm flood. I began to cry.

Still crying, I walked back to my clothes and put them on. I wanted to stop crying, but I just didn't seem able to turn off the waterworks. Then the shakes set in, making it worse. Vern ran up to me, still naked.

"They off, Gordie? They off me? They off me?"

He twirled in front of me like an insane dancer on a carnival stage.

"They off? Huh? Huh? They off me, Gordie?"

His eyes kept going past me, as wide and white as the eyes of a plaster horse on a merry-go-round.

I nodded that they were and just kept on crying. It seemed that crying was going to be my new career. I tucked my shirt in and then buttoned it all the way to the neck. I put on my socks and my sneakers. Little by little the tears began to slow down. Finally there was nothing left but a few hitches and moans, and then they stopped, too.

Chris walked over to me, wiping his mouth with a handful of elm leaves. His eyes were wide and mute and apologetic.

When we were all dressed we just stood there looking at each other for a moment, and then we began to climb the railroad embankment. I looked back once at the burst leech lying on top of the tromped-down bushes where we had danced and screamed and groaned them off. It looked deflated . . . but still ominous.

Fourteen years later I sold my first novel and made my first trip to New York. "It's going to be a three-day celebration," my new editor told me over the phone. "People slinging bullshit will be summarily shot." But of course it was three days of unmitigated bullshit.

While I was there I wanted to do all the standard out-of-towner things—see a stage show at the Radio City Music Hall, go to the top of the Empire State Building (fuck the World Trade Center; the building King Kong climbed in 1933 is always gonna be the tallest one in the world for me), visit Times Square by night. Keith, my editor, seemed more than pleased to show his city off. The last touristy thing we did was to take a ride on the Staten Island Ferry, and while leaning on the rail I happened to look down and see scores of used condoms floating on the mild swells. And I had a moment of almost total recall—or perhaps it was an actual incidence of time-travel. Either way, for one second I was literally *in* the past, pausing halfway up that embankment and looking back at the burst leech: dead, deflated . . . but still ominous.

Keith must have seen something in my face because he said: "Not very pretty, are they?"

I only shook my head, wanting to tell him not to apologize, wanting to tell him that you didn't have to come to the Apple and ride the ferry to see used rubbers, wanting to say: *The only reason anyone writes stories is so they can understand the past and get ready for some future mortality; that's why all the verbs in stories have -ed endings, Keith my good man, even the ones that sell millions of paperbacks. The only two useful artforms are religion and stories.*

I was pretty drunk that night, as you may have guessed.

What I did tell him was: "I was thinking of something else, that's all." The most important things are the hardest things to say.

22

We walked further down the tracks—I don't know just how far—and I was starting to think: *Well, okay, I'm going to be able to handle it, it's all over anyway, just a bunch of leeches, what the fuck;* I was still thinking it when waves of whiteness suddenly began to come over my sight and I fell down.

I must have fallen hard, but landing on the crossties was like plunging into a warm and puffy feather bed. Someone turned me over. The touch of hands was faint and unimportant. Their faces were disembodied balloons looking down at me from miles up. They looked the way the ref's face must look to a fighter who has been punched silly and is currently taking a ten-second rest on the canvas. Their words came in gentle oscillations, fading in and out.

". . . him?"

". . . be all . . ."

". . . if you think the sun . . ."

"Gordie, are you . . ."

Then I must have said something that didn't make much sense because they began to look *really* worried.

"We better take him back, man," Teddy said, and then the whiteness came over everything again.

When it cleared, I seemed to be all right. Chris was squat-

131

ting next to me, saying: "Can you hear me, Gordie? You there, man?"

"Yes," I said, and sat up. A swarm of black dots exploded in front of my eyes, and then went away. I waited to see if they'd come back, and when they didn't, I stood up.

"You scared the cheesly old shit outta me, Gordie," he said. "You want a drink of water?"

"Yeah."

He gave me his canteen, half-full of water, and I let three warm gulps roll down my throat.

"Why'd you faint, Gordie?" Vern asked anxiously.

"Made a bad mistake and looked at your face," I said.

"Eeee-eee-eeee!" Teddy cackled. "Fuckin Gordie! You wet!"

"You really okay?" Vern persisted.

"Yeah. Sure. It was . . . bad there for a minute. Thinking about those suckers."

They nodded soberly. We took five in the shade and then went on walking, me and Vern on one side of the tracks again, Chris and Teddy on the other. We figured we must be getting close.

23

We weren't as close as we thought, and if we'd had the brains to spend two minutes looking at a roadmap, we would have seen why. We knew that Ray Brower's corpse had to be near the Back Harlow Road, which dead-ends on the bank of the Royal River. Another trestle carries the GS&WM tracks across the Royal. So this is the way we figured: Once we got close to the Royal, we'd be getting close to the Back Harlow Road, where Billy and Charlie had been parked when they saw the boy. And since the Royal was only ten miles from the Castle River, we figured we had it made in the shade.

But that was ten miles as the crow flies, and the tracks didn't move on a straight line between the Castle and the Royal. Instead, they made a very shallow loop to avoid a hilly, crumbling region called The Bluffs. Anyway, we could have seen that loop quite clearly if we had looked on a map, and figured out that, instead of ten miles, we had about sixteen to walk.

Chris began to suspect the truth when noon had come and gone and the Royal still wasn't in sight. We stopped while he climbed a high pine tree and took a look around. He came down and gave us a simple enough report: it was going to be at least four in the afternoon before we got to the Royal, and we would only make it by then if we humped right along.

"Ah, *shit*!" Teddy cried. "So what're we gonna do now?"

We looked into each others' tired, sweaty faces. We were hungry and out of temper. The big adventure had turned into a long slog—dirty and sometimes scary. We would have been missed back home by now, too, and if Milo Pressman hadn't already called the cops on us, the engineer of the train crossing the trestle might have done it. We had been planning to hitchhike back to Castle Rock, but four o'clock was just three hours from dark, and *nobody* gives four kids on a back country road a lift after dark.

I tried to summon up the cool image of my deer, cropping at green morning grass, but even that seemed dusty and no good, no better than a stuffed trophy over the mantel in some guy's hunting lodge, the eyes sprayed to give them that phony lifelike shine.

Finally Chris said: "It's still closer out going ahead. Let's go."

He turned and started to walk along the tracks in his dusty sneakers, head down, his shadow only a puddle at his feet.

After a minute or so the rest of us followed him, strung out in Indian file.

24

In the years between then and the writing of this memoir, I've thought remarkably little about those two days in September, at least consciously. The associations the memories bring to the surface are as unpleasant as week-old river-corpses brought to the surface by cannonfire. As a result, I never really questioned our decision to walk down the tracks. Put another way, I've wondered sometimes about *what* we had decided to do but never how we did it.

But now a much simpler scenario comes to mind. I'm confident that if the idea *had* come up it would have been shot down—walking down the tracks would have seemed neater, *bosser,* as we said then. But if the idea had come up and *hadn't* been shot down in flames, none of the things which occurred later would have happened. Maybe Chris and Teddy and Vern would even be alive today. No, they didn't die in the woods or on the railroad tracks; nobody dies in this story except some bloodsuckers and Ray Brower, and if you want to be completely fair about it, he was dead before it even started. But it *is* true that, of the four of us who flipped coins to see who would go down to the Florida Market to get supplies, only the one who actually went is still alive. The Ancient Mariner at thirty-four, with you, Gentle Reader, in the role of Wedding Guest (at this point shouldn't you flip to the jacket photo to see if my eye holdeth you in its spell?). If you sense a certain flipness on my part, you're right—but maybe I have cause. At an age when all four of us would be considered too young and immature to be President, three of us are dead. And if small events really do echo up larger and larger through time, yes, maybe if we had done the simple thing and simply hitched into Harlow, they would still be alive today.

We could have hooked a ride all the way up Route 7 to the Shiloh Church, which stood at the intersection of the highway and the Back Harlow Road (at least until 1967, when it was levelled by a fire attributed to a tramp's smouldering cigarette butt). With reasonable luck we could have gotten to where the body was by sundown of the previous day.

But the idea wouldn't have lived. It wouldn't have been shot down with tightly buttressed arguments and debating society rhetoric, but with grunts and scowls and farts and raised middle fingers. The verbal part of the discussion would have been carried forward with such trenchant and sparkling contributions as "Fuck no," "That sucks," and that old reliable standby, "Did your mother ever have any kids that lived?"

Unspoken—maybe it was too fundamental to be spoken—was the idea that this was a *big* thing. It wasn't screwing around with firecrackers or trying to look through the knothole in the back of the girls' privy at Harrison State Park. This was something on a par with getting laid for the first time, or going into the Army, or buying your first bottle of legal liquor—just bopping into that state store, if you can dig it, selecting a bottle of good Scotch, showing the clerk your draft-card and driver's license, then walking out with a grin on your face and that brown bag in your hand, member of a club with just a few more rights and privileges than our old treehouse with the tin roof.

There's a high ritual to all fundamental events, the rites of passage, the magic corridor where the change happens. Buying the condoms. Standing before the minister. Raising your hand and taking the oath. Or, if you please, walking down the railroad tracks to meet a fellow your own age halfway, the same as I'd walk halfway over to Pine Street to meet Chris if he was coming over to my house, or the way Teddy would walk halfway down Gates Street to meet me if I was going to his. It seemed right to do it this way, because the rite of passage *is* a magic corridor and so we always provide an aisle—it's what you walk down when you get married, what they carry you down when you get buried. Our corridor was those twin rails, and we walked between them, just hopping along toward whatever this was supposed to mean. You don't hitchhike your way to a thing like that, maybe. And maybe we thought it was also right that it should have turned out to be harder than we had expected. Events surrounding our hike had turned it into what we had suspected it was all along: serious business.

What we *didn't* know as we walked around The Bluffs was that Billy Tessio, Charlie Hogan, Jack Mudgett, Norman "Fuzzy" Bracowicz, Vince Desjardins, Chris's older brother Eyeball, and Ace Merrill himself were all on their way to take a look at the body themselves—in a weird kind of way, Ray Brower had become famous, and our secret had turned into a regular roadshow. They were piling into Ace's chopped and channelled '52 Ford and Vince's pink '54 Studebaker even as we started on the last leg of our trip.

Billy and Charlie had managed to keep their enormous secret for just about thirty-six hours. Then Charlie spilled it to Ace while they were shooting pool, and Billy had spilled it to Jack Mudgett while they were fishing for steelies from the Boom Road Bridge. Both Ace and Jack had sworn solemnly on their mothers' names to keep the secret, and that was how everybody in their gang knew about it by noon. Guess you could tell what those assholes thought about their mothers.

They all congregated down at the pool hall, and Fuzzy Bracowicz advanced a theory (which you have heard before, Gentle Reader) that they could all become heroes—not to mention instant radio and TV personalities—by "discovering" the body. All they had to do, Fuzzy maintained, was to take two cars with a lot of fishing gear in the trunks. After they found the body, their story would be a hundred per cent. We was just plannin to take a few pickerel out of the Royal River, officer. Heh-heh-heh. Look what we found.

They were burning up the road from Castle Rock to the Back Harlow area just as we started to finally get close.

25

Clouds began to build in the sky around two o'clock, but at first none of us took them seriously. It hadn't rained since the early days of July, so why should it rain now? But they kept building to the south of us, up and up and up, thunderheads in great pillars as purple as bruises, and they began to move slowly our way. I looked at them closely, checking for that membrane beneath that means it's already raining twenty miles away, or fifty. But there was no rain yet. The clouds were still just building.

Vern got a blister on his heel and we stopped and rested while he packed the back of his left sneaker with moss stripped from the bark of an old oak tree.

"Is it gonna rain, Gordie?" Teddy asked.

"I think so."

"Pisser!" he said, and sighed. "The pisser good end to a pisser good day."

I laughed and he tipped me a wink.

We started to walk again, a little more slowly now out of respect for Vern's hurt foot. And in the hour between two and three, the quality of the day's light began to change, and we knew for sure that rain was coming. It was just as hot as ever, and even more humid, but we knew. And the birds did. They seemed to appear from nowhere and swoop across the sky, chattering and crying shrilly to each other. And the light. From a steady, beating brightness it seemed to evolve into something filtered, almost pearly. Our shadows, which had begun to grow long again, also grew fuzzy and ill-defined. The sun had begun to sail in and out through the thickening decks of clouds, and the southern sky had gone a coppery shade. We watched the thunderheads lumber closer, fascinated by their size and their mute threat. Every now and then it seemed that a giant flashbulb had gone off inside one of them, turning their purplish, bruised color momentarily to a light gray. I saw a jagged fork of lightning lick down from the underside of the closest. It was bright enough to print a blue tattoo on my retinas. It was followed by a long, shaking blast of thunder.

We did a little bitching about how we were going to get caught out in the rain, but only because it was the expected thing—of course we were all looking forward to it. It would be cold and refreshing . . . and leech-free.

At a little past three-thirty, we saw running water through a break in the trees.

"That's it!" Chris yelled jubilantly. "That's the Royal!"

We began to walk faster, taking our second wind. The storm was getting close now. The air began to stir, and it seemed that the temperature dropped ten degrees in a space of seconds. I looked down and saw that my shadow had disappeared entirely.

We were walking in pairs again, each two watching a side of the railroad embankment. My mouth was dry, throbbing with a sickish tension. The sun sailed behind another cloudbank and this time it didn't come back out. For a moment the bank's edges were embroidered with gold, like a cloud in an Old Testament Bible illustration, and then the wine-colored, dragging belly of the thunderhead blotted out all traces of the sun. The day became gloomy—the clouds were rapidly eating up the last of the blue. We could smell the river so clearly that we might have been horses—or perhaps it was the smell of rain impending in the air as well. There was an ocean above us, held in by a thin sac that might rupture and let down a flood at any second.

I kept trying to look into the underbrush, but my eyes were continually drawn back to that turbulent, racing sky; in its deepening colors you could read whatever doom you liked: water, fire, wind, hail. The cool breeze became more insistent, hissing in the firs. A sudden impossible bolt of lightning flashed down, seemingly from directly overhead, making me cry out and clap my hands to my eyes. God had taken my picture, a little kid with his shirt tied around his waist, duck-bumps on his bare chest and cinders on his cheeks. I heard the rending fall of some big tree not sixty yards away. The crack of thunder which followed made me cringe. I wanted to be at home reading a good book in a safe place . . . like down in the potato cellar.

"Jeezis!" Vern screamed in a high, fainting voice. "Oh my Jeezis Chrise, lookit *that*!"

I looked in the direction Vern was pointing and saw a blue-white fireball bowling its way up the lefthand rail of the GS&WM tracks, crackling and hissing for all the world like a scalded cat. It hurried past us as we turned to watch it go, dumbfounded, aware for the first time that such things could exist. Twenty feet beyond us it made a sudden—*pop!!*—and just disappeared, leaving a greasy smell of ozone behind.

"What am I *doin* here, anyway?" Teddy muttered.

"What a pisser!" Chris exclaimed happily, his face upturned. "This is gonna be a pisser like you wouldn't *believe*!" But I was with Teddy. Looking up at that sky gave me a dismaying sense of vertigo. It was more like looking into some deeply mysterious marbled gorge. Another lightning-bolt crashed down, making us duck. This time the ozone smell was hotter, more urgent. The following clap of thunder came with no perceptible pause at all.

My ears were still ringing from it when Vern began to screech triumphantly: *"THERE! THERE HE IS! RIGHT THERE! I SEE HIM!"*

I can see Vern right this minute, if I want to—all I have to do is sit back for a minute and close my eyes. He's standing there on the lefthand rail like an explorer on the prow of his ship, one hand shielding his eyes from the silver stroke of lightning that has just come down, the other extended and pointing.

We ran up beside him and looked. I was thinking to myself: *Vern's imagination just ran away with him, that's all. The suckers, the heat, now this storm . . . his eyes are dealing wild cards, that's all.* But that wasn't what it was, although there was a split second when I wanted it to be. In that split second I knew I never wanted to see a corpse, not even a runover woodchuck.

In the place where we were standing, early spring rains had washed part of the embankment away, leaving a gravelly, uncertain four-foot drop-off. The railroad maintenance crews had either not yet gotten around to it in their yellow diesel-operated repair carts, or it had happened so recently it hadn't yet been reported. At the bottom of this washout was a marshy, mucky tangle of undergrowth that smelled bad. And sticking out of a wild clockspring of blackberry brambles was a single pale white hand.

Did any of us breathe? I didn't.

The breeze was now a wind—harsh and jerky, coming at us from no particular direction, jumping and whirling, slapping at our sweaty skins and open pores. I hardly noticed. I think part of my mind was waiting for Teddy to cry out *Paratroops over the side!,* and I thought if he did that I might just go crazy. It would have been better to see the whole body, all at once, but instead there was only that limp outstretched hand, horribly white, the fingers limply splayed, like the hand of a drowned boy. It told us the truth of the whole matter. It explained every graveyard in the world. The image of that hand came back to me every time I heard or read of an atrocity. Somewhere, attached to that hand, was the rest of Ray Brower.

Lightning flickered and stroked. Thunder ripped in behind each stroke as if a drag race had started over our heads.

"Sheeeee . . ." Chris said, the sound not quite a cuss word, not quite the country version of *shit* as it is pronounced around a slender stem of timothy grass when the baler breaks down— instead it was a long, tuneless syllable without meaning; a sigh that had just happened to pass through the vocal cords.

Vern was licking his lips in a compulsive sort of way, as if he had tasted some obscure new delicacy, a Howard Johnson's 29th flavor, Tibetan Sausage Rolls, Interstellar Escargot, something so weird that it excited and revolted him at the same time.

Teddy only stood and looked. The wind whipped his greasy, clotted hair first away from his ears and then back over them. His face was a total blank. I could tell you I saw something there, and perhaps I did, in hindsight . . . but not then.

There were black ants trundling back and forth across the hand.

A great whispering noise began to rise in the woods on either side of the tracks, as if the forest had just noticed we were there and was commenting on it. The rain had started.

Dime-sized drops fell on my head and arms. They struck the embankment, turning the fill dark for a moment—and then the color changed back again as the greedy dry ground sucked the moisture up.

Those big drops fell for maybe five seconds and then they stopped. I looked at Chris and he blinked back at me.

Then the storm came all at once, as if a shower chain had been pulled in the sky. The whispering sound changed to loud contention. It was as if we were being rebuked for our discovery, and it was frightening. Nobody tells you about the pathetic fallacy until you're in college . . . and even then I noticed that nobody but the total dorks completely believed it *was* a fallacy.

Chris jumped over the side of the washout, his hair already soaked and clinging to his head. I followed. Vern and Teddy came close behind, but Chris and I were first to reach the body of Ray Brower. He was face down. Chris looked into my eyes, his face set and stern—an adult's face. I nodded slightly, as if he had spoken aloud.

I think he was down here and relatively intact instead of up there between the rails and completely mangled because he was trying to get out of the way when the train hit him, knocking him head over heels. He had landed with his head pointed toward the tracks, arms over his head like a diver about to execute. He had landed in this boggy cup of land that was becoming a small swamp. His hair was a dark reddish color. The moisture in the air had made it curl slightly at the ends. There was blood in it, but not a great deal, not a grossout amount. The ants were grosser. He was wearing a solid color dark green tee-shirt and bluejeans. His feet were bare, and a few feet behind him, caught in tall blackberry brambles, I saw a pair of filthy low-topped Keds. For a moment I was puzzled—why was he here and his tennies there? Then I realized, and the realization was like a dirty punch below the belt. My wife, my kids, my friends—they all think that having an imagination like mine must be quite nice; aside from making all this dough, I can have a little mind-movie whenever things get dull. Mostly they're right. But every now and then it turns around and bites the shit out of you with these long teeth, teeth that have been filed to points like the teeth of a cannibal. You see things you'd just as soon not see, things that keep you awake until first light. I saw one of those things now, saw it with absolute clarity and certainty. He had been knocked spang out of his Keds. The train had knocked him out of his Keds just as it had knocked the life out of his body.

That finally rammed it all the way home for me. The kid was dead. The kid wasn't sick, the kid wasn't sleeping. The kid wasn't going to get up in the morning anymore or get the runs from eating too many apples or catch poison ivy or wear out the eraser on the end of his Ticonderoga No. 2 during a hard math test. The kid was dead; stone dead. The kid was never going to go out bottling with his friends in the spring, gunnysack over his shoulder to pick up the returnables the retreating snow uncovered. The kid wasn't going to wake up at two o'clock a.m. on the morning of November 1st this year, run to the bathroom, and vomit up a big glurt of cheap Holloween candy. The kid wasn't going to pull a single girl's braid in home room. The kid wasn't going to give a bloody nose, or get one. The kid was *can't, don't, won't, never, shouldn't, wouldn't, couldn't.* He was the side of the battery where the terminal says neg. The fuse you have to put a penny in. The wastebasket by the teacher's desk, which always smells of wood-shavings from the sharpener and dead orange peels from lunch. The haunted house outside of town where the windows are crashed out, the NO TRESPASSING signs whipped away across the fields, the attic full of bats, the cellar full of rats. The kid was dead, mister, ma'am, young sir, little miss. I could go on all day and never get it right about the distance between his bare feet on the ground and his dirty Keds hanging in the bushes. It was thirty-plus inches, it was a googol of light-years. The kid was disconnected from his Keds beyond all hope of reconciliation. He was dead.

We turned him face up into the pouring rain, the lightning, the steady crack of thunder.

There were ants and bugs all over his face and neck. They ran briskly in and out of the round collar of his tee-shirt. His eyes were open, but terrifyingly out of sync—one was rolled back so far that we could see only a tiny arc of iris; the other stared straight up into the storm. There was a dried froth of blood above his mouth and on his chin—from a bloody nose, I thought—and the right side of his face was lacerated and darkly bruised. Still, I thought, he didn't really look bad. I had once walked into a door my brother Dennis was shoving open, came off with bruises even worse than this kid's, *plus* the bloody nose, and still had two helpings of everything for supper after it happened.

Teddy and Vern stood behind us, and if there had been any sight at all left in that one upward-staring eye, I suppose we would have looked to Ray Brower like pallbearers in a horror movie.

A beetle came out of his mouth, trekked across his fuzzless cheek, stepped onto a nettle, and was gone.

"D'joo see that?" Teddy asked in a high, strange, fainting voice. "I bet he's fuckin *fulla* bugs! I bet his *brains're*—"

"Shut up, Teddy," Chris said, and Teddy did, looking relieved.

Lightning forked blue across the sky, making the boy's single eye light up. You could almost believe he was glad to be found, and found by boys his own age. His torso had swelled up and there was a faint gassy odor about him, like the smell of old farts.

I turned away, sure I was going to be sick, but my stomach was dry, hard, steady. I suddenly rammed two fingers down my throat, trying to *make* myself heave, needing to do it, as if I could sick it up and get rid of it. But my stomach only hitched a little and then was steady again.

The roaring downpour and the accompanying thunder had

completely covered the sound of cars approaching along the Back Harlow Road, which lay bare yards beyond this boggy tangle. It likewise covered the crackle-crunch of the underbrush as they blundered through it from the dead end where they had parked.

And the first we knew of them was Ace Merrill's voice raised above the tumult of the storm, saying: "Well what the fuck do you know about this?"

26

We all jumped like we had been goosed and Vern cried out— he admitted later that he thought, for just a second, that the voice had come from the dead boy.

On the far side of the boggy patch, where the woods took up again, masking the butt end of the road, Ace Merrill and Eyeball Chambers stood together, half-obscured by a pouring gray curtain of rain. They were both wearing red nylon high school jackets, the kind you can buy in the office if you're a regular student, the same kind they give away free to varsity sports players. Their d.a. haircuts had been plastered back against their skulls and a mixture of rainwater and Vitalis ran down their cheeks like ersatz tears.

"Sumbitch!" Eyeball said. "That's my little brother!"

Chris was staring at Eyeball with his mouth open. His shirt, wet, limp, and dark, was still tied around his skinny middle. His pack, stained a darker green by the rain, was hanging against his naked shoulderblades.

"You get away, Rich," he said in a trembling voice. "We found him. We got dibs."

"Fuck your dibs. We're gonna report 'im."

"No you're not," I said. I was suddenly furious with them,

turning up this way at the last minute. If we'd thought about it, we'd have known something like this was going to happen . . . but this was one time, somehow, that the older, bigger kids weren't going to steal it—to take something they wanted as if by divine right, as if their easy way was the right way, the only way. They had come in *cars*—I think that was what made me angriest. They had come in *cars*. "There's four of us, Eyeball. You just try."

"Oh, we'll *try,* don't worry," Eyeball said, and the trees shook behind him and Ace. Charlie Hogan and Vern's brother Billy stepped through them, cursing and wiping water out of their eyes. I felt a lead ball drop into my belly. It grew bigger as Jack Mudgett, Fuzzy Bracowicz, and Vince Desjardins stepped out behind Charlie and Billy.

"Here we all are," Ace said, grinning. "So you just—"

"*VERN!!*" Billy Tessio cried in a terrible, accusing, my-judgment-cometh-and-that-right-early voice. He made a pair of dripping fists. "You little sonofawhore! You was under the porch! Cock-*knocker!*"

Vern flinched.

Charlie Hogan waxed positively lyrical: "You little keyhole-peeping cunt-licking *bungwipe!* I ought to beat the living shit out of you!"

"Yeah? Well, try it!" Teddy brayed suddenly. His eyes were crazily alight behind his rainspotted glasses. "Come on, fightcha for 'im! Come on! Come on, big men!"

Billy and Charlie didn't need a second invitation. They started forward together and Vern flinched again—no doubt visualizing the ghosts of Beatings Past and Beatings Yet to Come. He flinched . . . but hung tough. He was with his friends, and we had been through a lot, and we hadn't got here in a couple of *cars*.

But Ace held Billy and Charlie back, simply by touching each of them on the shoulder.

"Now listen, you guys," Ace said. He spoke patiently, just as if we weren't all standing in a roaring rainstorm. "There's more of us than there are of you. We're bigger. We'll give you one chance to just blow away. I don't give a fuck where. Just make like a tree and leave."

Chris's brother giggled and Fuzzy clapped Ace on the back in appreciation of his great wit. The Sid Caesar of the j.d. set.

"Cause *we're* takin him." Ace smiled gently, and you could imagine him smiling that same gentle smile just before breaking his cue over the head of some uneducated punk who had made the terrible mistake of lipping off while Ace was lining up a shot. "If you go, we'll take him. If you stay, we'll beat the piss outta you and still take him. Besides," he added, trying to gild the thuggery with a little righteousness, "Charlie and Billy found him, so it's their dibs anyway."

"They was chicken!" Teddy shot back. "Vern told us about it! They was fuckin chicken right outta their fuckin minds!" He screwed his face up into a terrified, snivelling parody of Charlie Hogan. " 'I wish we never boosted that car! I wish we never went out on no Back Harlow Road to whack off a piece! Oh, Billee, what are we gonna do? Oh Billee, I think I just turned my Fruit of the Looms into a fudge factory! Oh Billee—' "

"That's it," Charlie said, starting forward again. His face was knotted with rage and sullen embarrassment. "Kid, whatever your name is, get ready to reach down your fuckin throat the next time you need to pick your nose."

I looked wildly down at Ray Brower. He stared calmly up into the rain with his one eye, below us but above it all. The thunder was still booming steadily, but the rain had begun to slack off.

"What do you say, Gordie?" Ace asked. He was holding Charlie lightly by the arm, the way an accomplished trainer would restrain a vicious dog. "You must have at least some of your brother's sense. Tell these guys to back off. I'll let Charlie beat up the foureyes el punko a little bit and then we all go about our business. What do you say?"

He was wrong to mention Denny. I had wanted to reason with him, to point out what Ace knew perfectly well, that we had every right to take Billy and Charlie's dibs since Vern had heard them giving said dibs away. I wanted to tell him how Vern and I had almost gotten run down by a freight train on the trestle which spans the Castle River. About Milo Pressman and his fearless—if stupid—sidekick, Chopper the Wonder-Dog. About the bloodsuckers, too. I guess all I really wanted to tell him was Come on, Ace, fair is fair. You know that. But he had to bring Denny into it, and what I heard coming out of my mouth instead of sweet reason was my own death-warrant: "Suck my fat one, you cheap dimestore hood."

Ace's mouth formed a perfect O of surprise—the expression was so unexpectedly prissy that under other circumstances it would have been a laff riot, so to speak. All of the others—on both sides of the bog—stared at me, dumbfounded.

Then Teddy screamed gleefully: "That's telling 'im, Gordie! Oh boy! Too cool!"

I stood numbly, unable to believe it. It was like some crazed understudy had shot onstage at the critical moment and declaimed lines that weren't even in the play. Telling a guy to suck was as bad as you could get without resorting to his mother. Out of the corner of my eye I saw that Chris had unshouldered his knapsack and was digging into it frantically, but I didn't get it—not then, anyway.

"Okay," Ace said softly. "Let's take em. Don't hurt nobody but the Lachance kid. I'm gonna break both his fuckin arms."

I went dead cold. I didn't piss myself the way I had on the

railroad trestle, but it must have been because I had nothing inside to let out. He meant it, you see; the years between then and now have changed my mind about a lot of things, but not about that. When Ace said he was going to break both of my arms, he absolutely meant it.

They started to walk toward us through the slackening rain. Jackie Mudgett took a switchknife out of his pocket and hit the chrome. Six inches of steel flicked out, dove-gray in the afternoon half-light. Vern and Teddy dropped suddenly into fighting crouches on either side of me. Teddy did so eagerly, Vern with a desperate, cornered grimace on his face.

The big kids advanced in a line, their feet splashing through the bog, which was now one big sludgy puddle because of the storm. The body of Ray Brower lay at our feet like a water-logged barrel. I got ready to fight . . . and that was when Chris fired the pistol he had hawked out of his old man's dresser.

KA-BLAM!

God, what a wonderful sound that was! Charlie Hogan jumped right up into the air. Ace Merrill, who had been staring straight at me, now jerked around and looked at Chris. His mouth made that O again. Eyeball looked absolutely astounded.

"Hey, Chris, that's Daddy's," he said. "You're gonna get the tar whaled out of you—"

"That's nothing to what you'll get," Chris said. His face was horribly pale, and all the life in him seemed to have been sucked upward, into his eyes. They blazed out of his face.

"Gordie was right, you're nothing but a bunch of cheap hoods. Charlie and Billy didn't want their fuckin dibs and you all know it. We wouldn't have walked way to fuck out here if they said they did. They just went someplace and puked the story up and let Ace Merrill do their thinkin for them." His voice rose to a scream. *"But you ain't gonna get him, do you hear me?"*

"Now listen," Ace said. "You better put that down before you take your foot off with it. You ain't got the sack to shoot a woodchuck." He began to walk forward again, smiling his gentle smile as he came. "You're just a sawed-off pint-sized pissy-assed little runt and I'm gonna make you *eat* that fuckin gun.

"Ace, if you don't stand still I'm going to shoot you. I swear to God."

"You'll go to *jayy-ail,*" Ace crooned, not even hesitating. He was still smiling. The others watched him with horrified fascination . . . much the same way as Teddy and Vern and I were looking at Chris. Ace Merrill was the hardest case for miles around and I didn't think Chris could bluff him down. And what did that leave? Ace didn't think a twelve-year-old punk would actually shoot him. I thought he was wrong; I thought Chris would shoot Ace before he let Ace take his father's pistol away from him. In those few seconds I was sure there was going to be bad trouble, the worst I'd ever known. Killing trouble, maybe. And all of it over who got dibs on a dead body.

Chris said softly, with great regret: "Where do you want it, Ace? Arm or leg? I can't pick. You pick for me."

And Ace stopped.

27

His face sagged, and I saw sudden terror on it. It was Chris's tone rather than his actual words, I think; the real regret that things were going to go from bad to worse. If it was a bluff, it's still the best I've ever seen. The other big kids were totally convinced; their faces were squinched up as if someone had just touched a match to a cherry-bomb with a short fuse.

Ace slowly got control of himself. The muscles in his face tightened again, his lips pressed together, and he looked at Chris the way you'd look at a man who has made a serious business proposition—to merge with your company, or handle your line of credit, or shoot your balls off. It was a waiting, almost curious expression, one that made you know that the terror was either gone or tightly lidded. Ace had recomputed the odds on not getting shot and had decided that they weren't as much in his favor as he had thought. But he was still dangerous—maybe more than before. Since then I've thought it was the rawest piece of brinkmanship I've ever seen. Neither of them was bluffing, they both meant business.

"All right," Ace said softly, speaking to Chris. "But I know how you're going to come out of this, motherfuck."

"No you don't," Chris said.

"You little prick!" Eyeball said loudly. "You're gonna wind up in traction for this!"

"Bite my bag," Chris told him.

With an inarticulate sound of rage Eyeball started forward and Chris put a bullet into the water about ten feet in front of him. It kicked up a splash. Eyeball jumped back, cursing.

"Okay, now what?" Ace asked.

"Now you guys get into your cars and bomb on back to Castle Rock. After that I don't care. But you ain't getting him." He touched Ray Brower lightly, almost reverently, with the toe of one sopping sneaker. "You dig me?"

"But we'll get *you*," Ace said. He was starting to smile again. "Don't you know that?"

"You might. You might not."

"We'll get you hard," Ace said, smiling. "We'll hurt you.

I can't believe you don't *know* that. We'll put you all in the fuckin hospital with fuckin ruptures. Sincerely."

"Oh, why don't you go home and fuck your mother some more? I hear she loves the way you do it."

Ace's smile froze. "I'll kill you for that. Nobody ranks my mother."

"I heard your mother fucks for bucks," Chris informed him, and as Ace began to pale, as his complexion began to approach Chris's own ghastly whiteness, he added: "In fact, I heard she throws blowjobs for jukebox nickels. I heard—"

Then the storm came back, viciously, all at once. Only this time it was hail instead of rain. Instead of whispering or talking, the woods now seemed alive with hokey B-movie jungle drums—it was the sound of big icy hailstones honking off treetrunks. Stinging pebbles began to hit my shoulders—it felt as if some sentient, malevolent force were throwing them. Worse than that, they began to strike Ray Brower's upturned face with an awful splatting sound that reminded us of him again, of his terrible and unending patience.

Vern caved in first, with a wailing scream. He fled up the embankment in huge, gangling strides. Teddy held out a minute longer, then ran after Vern, his hands held up over his head. On their side, Vince Desjardins floundered back under some nearby trees and Fuzzy Bracowicz joined him. But the others stood pat, and Ace began to grin again.

"Stick with me, Gordie," Chris said in a low, shaky voice. "Stick with me, man."

"I'm right here."

"Go on, now," Chris said to Ace, and he was able, by some magic, to get the shakiness out of his voice. He sounded as if he were instructing a stupid infant.

"We'll get you," Ace said. "We're not going to forget it, if that's what you're thinking. This is big time, baby."

"That's fine. You just go on and do your getting another day."

"We'll fuckin ambush you, Chambers. We'll—"

"Get out!" Chris screamed, and levelled the gun. Ace stepped back.

He looked at Chris a moment longer, nodded, then turned around. "Come on," he said to the others. He looked back over his shoulder at Chris and me once more. "Be seeing you."

They went back into the screen of trees between the bog and the road. Chris and I stood perfectly still in spite of the hail that was welting us, reddening our skins, and piling up all around us like summer snow. We stood and listened and above the crazy calypso sound of the hail hitting the treetrunks we heard two cars start up.

"Stay right here," Chris told me, and he started across the bog.

"Chris!" I said, panicky.

"I got to. Stay here."

It seemed he was gone a very long time. I became convinced that either Ace or Eyeball had lurked behind and grabbed him. I stood my ground with nobody but Ray Brower for company and waited for somebody—anybody—to come back. After a while, Chris did.

"We did it," he said. "They're gone."

"You sure?"

"Yeah. Both cars." He held his hands up over his head, locked together with the gun between them, and shook the double fist in a wry championship gesture. Then he dropped them and smiled at me. I think it was the saddest scaredest smile I ever saw. " 'Suck my fat one'—whoever told you you had a fat one, Lachance?"

"Biggest one in four counties," I said. I was shaking all over.

We looked at each other warmly for a second, and then, maybe embarrassed by what we were seeing, looked down together. A nasty thrill of fear shot through me, and the sudden *splash/splash* as Chris shifted his feet let me know that he had seen, too. Ray Brower's eyes had gone wide and white, starey and pupilless, like the eyes that look out at you from Grecian statuary. It only took a second to understand what had happened, but understanding didn't lessen the horror. His eyes had filled up with round white hailstones. Now they were melting and the water ran down his cheeks as if he were weeping for his own grotesque position—a tatty prize to be fought over by two bunches of stupid hick kids. His clothes were also white with hail. He seemed to be lying in his own shroud.

"Oh, Gordie, hey," Chris said shakily. "Say-hey, man. What a creepshow for him."

"I don't think he knows—"

"Maybe that *was* his ghost we heard. Maybe he knew this was gonna happen. What a fuckin creepshow, I'm sincere."

Branches crackled behind us. I whirled, sure they had flanked us, but Chris went back to contemplating the body after one short, almost casual glance. It was Vern and Teddy, their jeans soaked black and plastered to their legs, both of them grinning like dogs that have been sucking eggs.

"What are we gonna do, man?" Chris asked, and I felt a weird chill steal through me. Maybe he was talking to me, maybe he was . . . but he was still looking down at the body.

"We're gonna take him back, ain't we?" Teddy asked, puzzled. "We're gonna be heroes. Ain't that right?" He looked from Chris to me and back to Chris again.

Chris looked up as if startled out of a dream. His lip curled. He took big steps toward Teddy, planted both hands on Teddy's chest, and pushed him roughly backwards. Teddy stumbled, pinwheeled his arms for balance, then sat down with a soggy splash. He blinked up at Chris like a surprised muskrat. Vern was looking warily at Chris, as if he feared madness. Perhaps that wasn't far from the mark.

"You keep your trap shut," Chris said to Teddy. "Paratroops over the side my ass. You lousy rubber chicken."

"It was the *hail*!" Teddy cried out, angry and ashamed. "It wasn't those guys, Chris! I'm ascared of *storms*! I can't help it! I would have taken all of em on at once, I swear on my mother's name! But I'm ascared of *storms*! Shit! I can't help it!" He began to cry again, sitting there in the water.

"What about you?" Chris asked, turning to Vern. "Are you scared of storms, too?"

Vern shook his head vacuously, still astounded by Chris's rage. "Hey, man, I thought we was all runnin."

"You must be a mind-reader then, because you ran first."

Vern swallowed twice and said nothing.

Chris stared at him, his eyes sullen and wild. Then he turned to me. "Going to build him a litter, Gordie."

"If you say so, Chris."

"Sure! Like in Scouts." His voice had begun to climb into strange, reedy levels. "Just like in the fuckin Scouts. A litter—poles and shirts. Like in the handbook. Right, Gordie?"

"Yeah. If you want. But what if those guys—"

"*Fuck those guys!*" he screamed. "*You're all a bunch of chickens! Fuck off, creeps!*"

"Chris, they could call the Constable. To get back at us."

"*He's ours and we're gonna take him OUT!*"

"Those guys would say anything to get us in dutch," I told him. My words sounded thin, stupid, sick with the flu. "Say anything and then lie each other up. You know how people can get other people in trouble telling lies, man. Like with the milk-mo—"

"*I DON'T CARE!*" he screamed, and lunged at me with his fists up. But one of his feet struck Ray Brower's ribcage with a soggy thump, making the body rock. He tripped and fell full-length and I waited for him to get up and maybe punch me in the mouth but instead he lay where he had fallen, head pointing toward the embankment, arms stretched out over his head like a diver about to execute, in the exact posture Ray Brower had been in when we found him. I looked wildly at Chris's feet to make sure his sneakers were still on. Then he began to cry and scream, his body bucking in the muddy water, splashing it around, fists drumming up and down in it, head twisting from side to side. Teddy and Vern were staring at him, agog, because nobody had ever seen Chris Chambers cry. After a moment or two I walked back to the embankment, climbed it, and sat down on one of the rails. Teddy and Vern followed me. And we sat there in the rain, not talking, looking like those three Monkeys of Virtue they sell in dime-stores and those sleazy gift-shops that always look like they are tottering on the edge of bankruptcy.

28

It was twenty minutes before Chris climbed the embankment to sit down beside us. The clouds had begun to break. Spears of sun came down through the rips. The bushes seemed to have gone three shades darker green in the last forty-five minutes. He was mud all the way up one side and down the other. His hair was standing up in muddy spikes. The only clean parts of him were the whitewashed circles around his eyes.

"You're right, Gordie," he said. "Nobody gets last dibs. Goocher all around, huh?"

I nodded. Five minutes passed. No one said anything. And I happened to have a thought—just in case they *did* call Bannerman. I went back down the embankment and over to where Chris had been standing. I got down on my knees and began to comb carefully through the water and marshgrass with my fingers.

"What you doing?" Teddy asked, joining me.

"It's to your left, I think," Chris said, and pointed.

I looked there and after a minute or two I found both shell casings. They winked in the fresh sunlight. I gave them to Chris. He nodded and stuffed them into a pocket of his jeans.

"Now we go," Chris said.

"Hey, come *on*!" Teddy yelled, in real agony. "I wanna *take* 'im!"

"Listen, dummy," Chris said, "if we take him back we could all wind up in the reformatory. It's like Gordie says. Those guys could make up any story they wanted to. What if they said *we* killed him, huh? How would you like that?"

"I don't give a damn," Teddy said sulkily. Then he looked at us with absurd hope. "Besides, we might only get a couple of months or so. As excessories. I mean, we're only twelve fuckin years old, they ain't gonna put us in Shawshank."

Chris said softly: "You can't get in the Army if you got a record, Teddy."

I was pretty sure that was nothing but a bald-faced lie— but somehow this didn't seem the time to say so. Teddy just looked at Chris for a long time, his mouth trembling. Finally he managed to squeak out: "No shit?"

"Ask Gordie."

He looked at me hopefully.

"He's right," I said, feeling like a great big turd. "He's right, Teddy. First thing they do when you volunteer is to check your name through R&I."

"Holy *God*!"

"We're gonna shag ass back to the trestle," Chris said. "Then we'll get off the tracks and come into Castle Rock from the other direction. If people ask where we were, we'll say we went campin up on Brickyard Hill and got lost."

"Milo Pressman knows better," I said. "That creep at the Florida Market does, too."

"Well, we'll say Milo scared us and that's when we decided to go up on the Brickyard."

I nodded. That might work. If Vern and Teddy could remember to stick to it.

"What about if our folks get together?" Vern asked.

"You worry about it if you want," Chris said. "My dad'll still be juiced up."

"Come on, then," Vern said, eyeing the screen of trees between us and the Back Harlow Road. He looked like he expected Bannerman, along with a brace of bloodhounds, to come crashing through at any moment. "Let's get while the gettin's good."

We were all on our feet now, ready to go. The birds were singing like crazy, pleased with the rain and the shine and the worms and just about everything in the world, I guess. We all turned around, as if pulled on strings, and looked back at Ray Brower.

He was lying there, alone again. His arms had flopped out when we turned him over and now he was sort of spread-eagled, as if to welcome the sunshine. For a moment it seemed all right, a more natural deathscene than any ever constructed for a viewing-room audience by a mortician. Then you saw the bruise, the caked blood on the chin and under the nose, and the way the corpse was beginning to bloat. You saw that the bluebottles had come out with the sun and that they were circling the body, buzzing indolently. You remembered that gassy smell, sickish but dry, like farts in a closed room. He was a boy our age, he was dead, and I rejected the idea that anything about it could be natural; I pushed it away with horror.

"Okay," Chris said, and he meant to be brisk but his voice came out of his throat like a handful of dry bristles from an old whiskbroom. "Double-time."

We started to almost-trot back the way we had come. We

didn't talk. I don't know about the others, but I was too busy thinking to talk. There were things that bothered me about the body of Ray Brower—they bothered me then and they bother me now.

A bad bruise on the side of his face, a scalp laceration, a bloody nose. No more—at least, no more visible. People walk away from bar-fights in worse condition and go right on drinking. Yet the train *must* have hit him; why else would his sneakers be off his feet that way? And how come the engineer hadn't seen him? Could it be that the train had hit him hard enough to toss him but not to kill him? I thought that, under just the right combination of circumstances, that could have happened. Had the train hit him a hefty, teeth-rattling sideswipe as he tried to get out of the way? Hit him and knocked him in a flying, backwards somersault over that caved-in banking? Had he perhaps lain awake and trembling in the dark for hours, not just lost now but disoriented as well, cut off from the world? Maybe he had died of fear. A bird with crushed tailfeathers once died in my cupped hands in just that way. Its body trembled and vibrated lightly, its beak opened and closed, its dark, bright eyes stared up at me. Then the vibration quit, the beak froze half-open and the black eyes became lackluster and uncaring. It could have been that way with Ray Brower. He could have died because he was simply too frightened to go on living.

But there was another thing, and that bothered me most of all, I think. He had started off to go berrying. I seemed to remember the news reports saying he'd been carrying a pot to put his berries in. When we got back I went to the library and looked it up in the newspapers just to be sure, and I was right. He'd been berrying, and he'd had a pail, or a pot—something like that. But we hadn't found it. We found him, and we found his sneakers. He must have thrown it away somewhere between Chamberlain and the boggy patch of ground in Harlow where he died. He perhaps clutched it even tighter at first, as though it linked him to home and safety. But as his fear grew, and with it that sense of being utterly alone, with no chance of rescue except for whatever he could do by himself, as the real cold terror set in, he maybe threw it away into the woods on one side of the tracks or the other, hardly even noticing it was gone.

I've thought of going back and looking for it—how does that strike you for morbid? I've thought of driving to the end of the Back Harlow Road in my almost new Ford van and getting out of it some bright summer morning, all by myself, my wife and children far off in another world where, if you turn a switch, lights come on in the dark. I've thought about how it would be. Pulling my pack out of the back and resting it on the customized van's rear bumper while I carefully remove my shirt and tie it around my waist. Rubbing my chest and shoulders with Muskol insect repellent and then crashing through the woods to where that boggy place was, the place where we found him. Would the grass grow up yellow there, in the shape of his body? Of course not, there would be no sign, but still you wonder, and you realize what a thin film there is between your rational man costume—the writer with leather elbow-patches on his corduroy jacket—and the capering, Gorgon myths of childhood. Then climbing the embankment, now overgrown with weeds, and walking slowly beside the rusted tracks and rotted ties toward Chamberlain.

Stupid fantasy. An expedition looking for a twenty-year-old blueberry bucket, which was probably cast deep into the woods or plowed under by a bulldozer readying a half-acre plot for a tract house or so deeply overgrown by weeds and brambles it had become invisible. But I feel sure it is still there, somewhere along the old discontinued GS&WM line, and at times the urge to go and look is almost a frenzy. It usually comes early in the morning, when my wife is showering and the kids are watching *Batman* and *Scooby-Doo* on channel 38 out of Boston, and I am feeling the most like the pre-adolescent Gordon Lachance that once strode the earth, walking and talking and occasionally crawling on his belly like a reptile. That boy was *me,* I think. And the thought which follows, chilling me like a dash of cold water, is: *Which boy do you mean?*

Sipping a cup of tea, looking at sun slanting through the kitchen windows, hearing the TV from one end of the house and the shower from the other, feeling the pulse behind my eyes that means I got through one beer too many the night before, I feel sure I could find it. I would see clear metal winking through rust, the bright summer sun reflecting it back to my eyes. I would go down the side of the embankment, push aside the grasses that had grown up and twined toughly around its handle, and then I would . . . what? Why, simply pull it out of time. I would turn it over and over in my hands, wondering at the feel of it, marvelling at the knowledge that the last person to touch it had been long years in his grave. Suppose there was a note in it? *Help me, I'm lost.* Of course there wouldn't be—boys don't go out to pick blueberries with paper and pencil—but just suppose. I imagine the awe I'd feel would be as dark as an eclipse. Still, it's mostly just the idea of holding that pail in my two hands, I guess—as much a symbol of my living as his dying, proof that I really do know which boy it was—which boy of the five of us. Holding it. Reading every year in its cake of rust and the fading of its bright shine. Feeling it, trying to understand the suns that shone on it, the rains that fell on it, and the snows that covered it. And to wonder where I was when each thing happened to it in its lonely place, where I was, what I was doing, who I was loving, how I was getting along, where I was. I'd hold it, read it, feel it . . . and look at my own face in whatever reflection might be left. Can you dig it?

29

We got back to Castle Rock a little past five o'clock on Sunday morning, the day before Labor Day. We had walked all night. Nobody complained, although we all had blisters and were all ravenously hungry. My head was throbbing with a killer headache, and my legs felt twisted and burning with fatigue. Twice we had to scramble down the embankment to get out of the way of freights. One of them was going our way, but moving far too fast to hop. It was seeping daylight when we got to the trestle spanning the Castle again. Chris looked at it, looked at the river, looked back at us.

"Fuck it. I'm walking across. If I get hit by a train I won't have to watch out for fuckin Ace Merrill."

We all walked across it—plodded might be the better verb. No train came. When we got to the dump we climbed the fence (no Milo and no Chopper, not this early, and not on a Sunday morning) and went directly to the pump. Vern primed it and we all took turns sticking our heads under the icy flow, slapping the water over our bodies, drinking until we could hold no more. Then we had to put our shirts on again because the morning seemed chilly. We walked—limped—back into town and stood for a moment on the sidewalk in front of the vacant lot. We looked at our treehouse so we wouldn't have to look at each other.

"Well," Teddy said at last, "seeya in school on Wednesday. I think I'm gonna sleep until then."

"Me too," Vern said. "I'm too pooped to pop."

Chris whistled tunelessly through his teeth and said nothing.

"Hey, man," Teddy said awkwardly. "No hard feelins, okay?"

"No," Chris said, and suddenly his somber, tired face broke into a sweet and sunny grin. "We did it, didn't we? We did the bastard."

"Yeah," Vern said. "You're fuckin-A. Now Billy's gonna do *me*."

"So what?" Chris said. "Richie's gonna tool up on me and Ace is probably gonna tool up on Gordie and somebody else'll tool up on Teddy. But we *did* it."

"That's right," Vern said. But he still sounded unhappy.

Chris looked at me. "We did it, didn't we?" he asked softly. "It was worth it, wasn't it?"

"Sure it was," I said.

"Fuck this," Teddy said in his dry I'm-losing-interest way. "You guys sound like fuckin *Meet the Press*. Gimme some skin, man. I'm gonna toot home and see if Mom's got me on the Ten Most Wanted List."

We all laughed, Teddy gave us his surprised Oh-Lord-what-now look, and we gave him skin. Then he and Vern started off in their direction and I should have gone in mine . . . but I hesitated for a second.

"Walk with you," Chris offered.

"Sure, okay."

We walked a block or so without talking. Castle Rock was awesomely quiet in the day's first light, and I felt an almost holy tiredness-is-slipping-away sort of feeling. We were awake and the whole world was asleep and I almost expected to turn the corner and see my deer standing at the far end of Carbine Street, where the GS&WM tracks pass through the mill's loading yard.

Finally Chris spoke. "They'll tell," he said.

163

"You bet they will. But not today or tomorrow, if that's what you're worried about. It'll be a long time before they tell, I think. Years, maybe."

He looked at me, surprised.

"They're scared, Chris. Teddy especially, that they won't take him in the Army. But Vern's scared, too. They'll lose some sleep over it, and there's gonna be times this fall when it's right on the tips of their tongues to tell somebody, but I don't think they will. And then . . . you know what? It sounds fucking crazy, but . . . I think they'll almost forget it ever happened."

He was nodding slowly. "I didn't think of it just like that. You see through people, Gordie."

"Man, I wish I did."

"You do, though."

We walked another block in silence.

"I'm never gonna get out of this town," Chris said, and sighed. "When you come back from college on summer vacation, you'll be able to look me and Vern and Teddy up down at Sukey's after the seven-to-three shift's over. If you want to. Except you'll probably never want to." He laughed a creepy laugh.

"Quit jerking yourself off," I said, trying to sound tougher than I felt—I was thinking about being out there in the woods, about Chris saying: *And maybe I took it to old lady Simons and told her, and maybe the money was all there but I got a three-day vacation* anyway, *because the money never showed up. And maybe the next week old lady Simons had this brand-new skirt on when she came to school . . .* The look. The look in his eyes.

"No jerkoff, daddy-O," Chris said.

I rubbed my first finger against my thumb. "This is the world's smallest violin playing 'My Heart Pumps Purple Piss for You.' "

"He was *ours*," Chris said, his eyes dark in the morning light.

We had reached the corner of my street and we stopped there. It was quarter past six. Back toward town we could see the Sunday *Telegram* truck pulling up in front of Teddy's uncle's stationery shop. A man in bluejeans and a tee-shirt threw off a bundle of papers. They bounced upside down on the sidewalk, showing the color funnies (always Dick Tracy and Blondie on the first page). Then the truck drove on, its driver intent on delivering the outside world to the rest of the whistlestops up the line—Otisfield, Norway-South Paris, Waterford, Stoneham. I wanted to say something more to Chris and didn't know how to.

"Gimme some skin, man," he said, sounding tired.

"Chris—"

"Skin."

I gave him some skin. "I'll see you."

He grinned—that same sweet, sunny grin. "Not if I see you first, fuckface."

He walked off, still laughing, moving easily and gracefully, as though he didn't hurt like me and have blisters like me and like he wasn't lumped and bumped with mosquito and chigger and blackfly bites like me. As if he didn't have a care in the world, as if he was going to some real boss place instead of just home to a three-room house (shack would have been closer to the truth) with no indoor plumbing and broken windows covered with plastic and a brother who was probably laying for him in the front yard. Even if I'd known the right thing to say, I probably couldn't have said it. Speech destroys the functions of love, I think—that's a hell of a thing for a writer to say, I guess, but I believe it to be true. If you speak to tell a deer you mean it no harm, it glides away with a single flip of its tail. The word is the harm. Love isn't what these asshole poets like McKuen want you to think it is. Love has teeth; they bite; the wounds never close. No word, no combination of words, can

165

close those lovebites. It's the other way around, that's the joke. If those wounds dry up, the words die with them. Take it from me. I've made my life from the words, and I know that is so.

30

The back door was locked so I fished the spare key out from under the mat and let myself in. The kitchen was empty, silent, suicidally clean. I could hear the hum the fluorescent bars over the sink made when I turned on the switch. It had been literally years since I had been up before my mother; I couldn't even remember the last time such a thing had happened.

I took off my shirt and put it in the plastic clothesbasket behind the washing machine. I got a clean rag from under the sink and sponged off with it—face, neck, pits, belly. Then I unzipped my pants and scrubbed my crotch—my testicles in particular—until my skin began to hurt. It seemed I couldn't get clean enough down there, although the red weal left by the bloodsucker was rapidly fading. I still have a tiny crescent-shaped scar there. My wife once asked about it and I told her a lie before I was even aware I meant to do so.

When I was done with the rag, I threw it away. It was filthy.

I got out a dozen eggs and scrambled six of them together. When they were semi-solid in the pan, I added a side dish of crushed pineapple and half a quart of milk. I was just sitting down to eat when my mother came in, her gray hair tied in a knot behind her head. She was wearing a faded pink bathrobe and smoking a Camel.

"Gordon, where have you been?"

"Camping," I said, and began to eat. "We started off in Vern's field and then went up the Brickyard Hill. Vern's mom said she would call you. Didn't she?"

"She probably talked to your father," she said, and glided past me to the sink. She looked like a pink ghost. The fluorescent bars were less than kind to her face; they made her complexion look almost yellow. She sighed . . . almost sobbed. "I miss Dennis most in the mornings," she said. "I always look in his room and it's always empty, Gordon. Always."

"Yeah, that's a bitch," I said.

"He always slept with his window open and the blankets . . . Gordon? Did you say something?"

"Nothing important, Mom."

". . . and the blankets pulled up to his chin," she finished. Then she just stared out the window, her back to me. I went on eating. I was trembling all over.

31

The story never did get out.

Oh, I don't mean that Ray Brower's body was never found; it was. But neither our gang nor their gang got the credit. In the end, Ace must have decided that an anonymous phone call was the safest course, because that's how the location of the corpse was reported. What I meant was that none of our parents ever found out what we'd been up to that Labor Day weekend.

Chris's dad was still drinking, just as Chris had said he would be. His mom had gone off to Lewiston to stay with her sister, the way she almost always did when Mr. Chambers was on a bender. She went and left Eyeball in charge of the younger kids. Eyeball had fulfilled his responsibility by going off with Ace and his j.d. buddies, leaving nine-year-old Sheldon, five-year-old Emery, and two-year-old Deborah to sink or swim on their own.

167

Teddy's mom got worried the second night and called Vern's mom. Vern's mom, who was also never going to do the game-show circuit, said we were still out in Vern's tent. She knew because she had seen a light on in there the night before. Teddy's mom said she sure hoped no one was smoking cigarettes in there and Vern's mom said it looked like a flashlight to her, and besides, she was sure that none of Vern's or Billy's friends smoked.

My dad asked me some vague questions, looking mildly troubled at my evasive answers, said we'd go fishing together sometime, and that was the end of it. If the parents had gotten together in the week or two afterward, everything would have fallen down . . . but they never did.

Milo Pressman never spoke up, either. My guess is that he thought twice about it being our word against his, and how we would all swear that he sicced Chopper on me.

So the story never came out—but that wasn't the end of it.

32

One day near the end of the month, while I was walking home from school, a black 1952 Ford cut into the curb in front of me. There was no mistaking that car. Gangster white-walls and spinner hubcaps, highrise chrome bumpers and Lucite death-knob with a rose embedded in it clamped to the steering wheel. Painted on the back deck was a deuce and a one-eyed jack. Beneath them, in Roman Gothic script, were the words WILD CARD.

The doors flew open; Ace Merrill and Fuzzy Bracowicz stepped out.

"Cheap hood, right?" Ace said, smiling his gentle smile. "My mother loves the way I do it to her, right?"

"We're gonna rack you, baby," Fuzzy said.

I dropped my schoolbooks on the sidewalk and ran. I was busting my buns but they caught me before I even made the end of the block. Ace hit me with a flying tackle and I went full-length on the paving. My chin hit the cement and I didn't just see stars; I saw whole constellations, whole nebulae. I was already crying when they picked me up, not so much from my elbows and knees, both pairs scraped and bleeding, or even from fear—it was vast, impotent rage that made me cry. Chris was right. He had been ours.

I twisted and turned and almost squiggled free. Then Fuzzy hoicked his knee into my crotch. The pain was amazing, incredible, nonpareil; it widened the horizons of pain from plain old wide screen to Vista Vision. I began to scream. Screaming seemed to be my best chance.

Ace punched me twice in the face, long and looping haymaker blows. The first one closed my left eye; it would be four days before I was really able to see out of that eye again. The second broke my nose with a crunch that sounded the way crispy cereal sounds inside your head when you chew. Then old Mrs. Chalmers came out on her porch with her cane clutched in one arthritis-twisted hand and a Herbert Tareyton jutting from one corner of her mouth. She began to bellow at them:

"Hi! Hi there, you boys! You stop that! Police! Poleeeece!"

"Don't let me see you around, dipshit," Ace said, smiling, and they let go of me and backed off. I sat up and then leaned over, cupping my wounded balls, sickly sure I was going to throw up and then die. I was still crying, too. But when Fuzzy started to walk around me, the sight of his pegged jeans-leg snuggered down over the top of his motorcycle boot brought all the fury back. I grabbed him and bit his calf through his jeans. I bit him just as hard as I could. Fuzzy began to do a little screaming of his own. He also began hopping around

169

on one leg, and, incredibly, he was calling me a dirty-fighter. I was watching him hop around and that was when Ace stamped down on my left hand, breaking the first two fingers. I heard them break. They didn't sound like crispy cereal. They sounded like pretzels. Then Ace and Fuzzy were going back to Ace's '52, Ace sauntering with his hands in his back pockets, Fuzzy hopping on one leg and throwing curses back over his shoulder at me. I curled up on the sidewalk, crying. Aunt Evvie Chalmers came down her walk, thudding her cane angrily as she came. She asked me if I needed the doctor. I sat up and managed to stop most of the crying. I told her I didn't.

"Bullshit," she bellowed—Aunt Evvie was deaf and bellowed everything. "I saw where that bully got you. Boy, your sweetmeats are going to swell up to the size of Mason jars."

She took me into her house, gave me a wet rag for my nose— it had begun to resemble a summer squash by then—and gave me a big cup of medicinal-tasting coffee that was somehow calming. She kept bellowing at me that she should call the doctor and I kept telling her not to. Finally she gave up and I walked home. Very slowly, I walked home. My balls weren't the size of Mason jars yet, but they were on their way.

My mom and dad got a look at me and wigged right out—I was sort of surprised that they noticed anything at all, to tell the truth. Who were the boys? Could I pick them out of a line-up? That from my father, who never missed *Naked City* and *The Untouchables*. I said I didn't think I could pick the boys out of a line-up. I said I was tired. Actually I think I was in shock—in shock and more than a little drunk from Aunt Evvie's coffee, which must have been at least sixty per cent VSOP brandy. I said I thought they were from some other town, or from "up the city"—a phrase everyone understood to mean Lewiston-Auburn.

They took me to Dr. Clarkson in the station wagon—Dr.

Clarkson, who is still alive today, was even then old enough to have quite possibly been on armchair-to-armchair terms with God. He set my nose and my fingers and gave my mother a prescription for painkiller. Then he got them out of the examining room on some pretext or other and came over to me, shuffling, head forward, like Boris Karloff approaching Igor.

"Who did it, Gordon?"

"I don't know, Dr. Cla—"

"You're lying."

"No, sir. Huh-uh."

His sallow cheeks began to flow with color. "Why should you protect the cretins who did this? Do you think they will respect you? They will laugh and call you stupid-fool! 'Oh,' they'll say, 'there goes the stupid-fool we beat up for kicks the other day. Ha-ha! Hoo-hoo! Har-de-har-har-har!'"

"I didn't know them. Really."

I could see his hands itching to shake me, but of course he couldn't do that. So he sent me out to my parents, shaking his white head and muttering about juvenile delinquents. He would no doubt tell his old friend God all about it that night over their cigars and sherry.

I didn't care if Ace and Fuzzy and the rest of those assholes respected me or thought I was stupid or never thought about me at all. But there was Chris to think of. His brother Eyeball had broken his arm in two places and had left his face looking like a Canadian sunrise. They had to set the elbow-break with a steel pin. Mrs. McGinn from down the road saw Chris staggering along the soft shoulder, bleeding from both ears and reading a Richie Rich comic book. She took him to the CMG Emergency Room where Chris told the doctor he had fallen down the cellar stairs in the dark.

"Right," the doctor said, every bit as disgusted with Chris

as Dr. Clarkson had been with me, and then he went to call Constable Bannerman.

While he did that from his office, Chris went slowly down the hall, holding the temporary sling against his chest so the arm wouldn't swing and grate the broken bones together, and used a nickel in the pay phone to call Mrs. McGinn—he told me later it was the first collect call he had ever made and he was scared to death that she wouldn't accept the charges—but she did.

"Chris, are you all right?" she asked.

"Yes, thank you," Chris said.

"I'm sorry I couldn't stay with you, Chris, but I had pies in the—"

"That's all right, Missus McGinn," Chris said. "Can you see the Buick in our dooryard?" The Buick was the car Chris's mother drove. It was ten years old and when the engine got hot it smelled like frying Hush Puppies.

"It's there," she said cautiously. Best not to mix in too much with the Chamberses. Poor white trash; shanty Irish.

"Would you go over and tell Mamma to go downstairs and take the lightbulb out of the socket in the cellar?"

"Chris, I really, my pies—"

"Tell her," Chris said implacably, "to do it right away. Unless she maybe wants my brother to go to jail."

There was a long, long pause and then Mrs. McGinn agreed. She asked no questions and Chris told her no lies. Constable Bannerman did indeed come out to the Chambers house, but Richie Chambers didn't go to jail.

Vern and Teddy took their lumps, too, although not as bad as either Chris or I. Billy was laying for Vern when Vern got home. He took after him with a stovelength and hit him hard enough to knock him unconscious after only four or five good licks. Vern was no more than stunned, but Billy got scared he might have killed him and stopped. Three of them caught

Teddy walking home from the vacant lot one afternoon. They punched him out and broke his glasses. He fought them, but they wouldn't fight him when they realized he was groping after them like a blindman in the dark.

We hung out together at school looking like the remains of a Korean assault force. Nobody knew exactly what had happened, but everybody understood that we'd had a pretty serious run-in with the big kids and comported ourselves like men. A few stories went around. All of them were wildly wrong.

When the casts came off and the bruises healed, Vern and Teddy just drifted away. They had discovered a whole new group of contemporaries that they could lord it over. Most of them were real wets—scabby, scrubby little fifth-grade assholes—but Vern and Teddy kept bringing them to the treehouse, ordering them around, strutting like Nazi generals.

Chris and I began to drop by there less and less frequently, and after awhile the place was theirs by default. I remember going up one time in the spring of 1961 and noticing that the place smelled like a shootoff in a haymow. I never went there again that I can recall. Teddy and Vern slowly became just two more faces in the halls or in three-thirty detention. We nodded and said hi. That was all. It happens. Friends come in and out of your life like busboys in a restaurant, did you ever notice that? But when I think of that dream, the corpses under the water pulling implacably at my legs, it seems right that it should be that way. Some people drown, that's all. It's not fair, but it happens. Some people drown.

33

Vern Tessio was killed in a housefire that swept a Lewiston apartment building in 1966—in Brooklyn and the Bronx, they call that sort of apartment building a slum tenement, I believe. The Fire Department said it started around two in the morning, and the entire building was nothing but cinders in the cellarhole by dawn. There had been a large drunken party; Vern was there. Someone fell asleep in one of the bedrooms with a live cigarette going. Vern himself, maybe, drifting off, dreaming of his pennies. They identified him and the four others who died by their teeth.

Teddy went in a squalid car crash. That was 1971, I think, or maybe it was early 1972. There used to be a saying when I was growing up: "If you go out alone you're a hero. Take somebody else with you and you're dogpiss." Teddy, who had wanted nothing but the service since the time he was old enough to want anything, was turned down by the Air Force and classified 4-F by the draft. Anyone who had seen his glasses and his hearing aid knew it was going to happen—anyone but Teddy. In his junior year at high school he got a three-day vacation from school for calling the guidance counselor a lying sack of shit. The g.o. had observed Teddy coming in every so often—like every day—and checking over his career-board for new service literature. He told Teddy that maybe he should think about another career, and that was when Teddy blew his stack.

He was held back a year for repeated absences, tardies, and the attendant flunked courses . . . but he *did* graduate. He had an ancient Chevrolet Bel Air, and he used to hang around the places where Ace and Fuzzy and the rest had hung around before him: the pool hall, the dance hall, Sukey's Tavern, which is closed now, and The Mellow Tiger, which isn't. He eventually got a job with the Castle Rock Public Works Department, filling up holes with hotpatch.

The crash happened over in Harlow. Teddy's Bel Air was full of his friends (two of them had been part of that group he and Vern took to bossing around way back in 1960), and they

174

were all passing around a couple of joints and a couple of bottles of Popov. They hit a utility pole and sheared it off and the Chevrolet rolled six times. One girl came out technically still alive. She lay for six months in what the nurses and orderlies at Central Maine General call the C&T Ward—Cabbages and Turnips. Then some merciful phantom pulled the plug on her respirator. Teddy Duchamp was posthumously awarded the Dogpiss of the Year Award.

Chris enrolled in the college courses in his second year of junior high—he and I both knew that if he waited any longer it would be too late; he would never catch up. Everyone jawed at him about it: his parents, who thought he was putting on airs, his friends, most of whom dismissed him as a pussy, the guidance counsellor, who didn't believe he could do the work, and most of all the teachers, who didn't approve of this duck-tailed, leather-jacketed, engineer-booted apparition who had materialized without warning in their classrooms. You could see that the sight of those boots and that many-zippered jacket offended them in connection with such high-minded subjects as algebra, Latin, and earth science; such attire was meant for the shop courses only. Chris sat among the well-dressed, vivacious boys and girls from the middle class families in Castle View and Brickyard Hill like some silent, brooding Grendel that might turn on them at any moment, produce a horrible roaring like the sound of dual glass-pack mufflers, and gobble them up, penny loafers, Peter Pan collars, button-down paisley shirts, and all.

He almost quit a dozen times that year. His father in particular hounded him, accusing Chris of thinking he was better than his old man, accusing Chris of wanting "to go up there to the college so you can turn me into a bankrupt." He once broke a Rhinegold bottle over the back of Chris's head and Chris wound up in the CMG Emergency Room again, where it took four stitches to close his scalp. His old friends, most of whom were now majoring in Smoking Area, catcalled him on the streets. The guidance counsellor huckstered him to take at least *some* shop courses so he wouldn't flunk the whole slate. Worst of all, of course, was just this: he'd been fucking off for the entire first seven years of his public education, and now the bill had come due with a vengeance.

We studied together almost every night, sometimes for as long as six hours at a stretch. I always came away from those sessions exhausted, and sometimes I came away frightened as well—frightened by his incredulous rage at just how murderously high that bill was. Before he could even begin to understand introductory algebra, he had to re-learn the fractions that he and Teddy and Vern had played pocket-pool through in the fifth grade. Before he could even begin to understand *Pater noster qui est in caelis,* he had to be told what nouns and prepositions and objects were. On the inside of his English grammar, neatly lettered, were the words FUCK GERUNDS. His compositional ideas were good and not badly organized, but his grammar was bad and he approached the whole business of punctuation as if with a shotgun. He wore out his copy of Warriner's and bought another in a Portland bookstore—it was the first hardcover book he actually owned, and it became a queer sort of Bible to him.

But by our junior year in high school, he had been accepted. Neither of us made top honors, but I came out seventh and Chris stood nineteenth. We were both accepted at the University of Maine, but I went to the Orono campus while Chris enrolled at the Portland campus. Pre-law, can you believe that? More Latin.

We both dated through high school, but no girl ever came between us. Does that sound like we went faggot? It would have to most of our old friends, Vern and Teddy included.

But it was only survival. We were clinging to each other in deep water. I've explained about Chris, I think; my reasons for clinging to him were less definable. His desire to get away from Castle Rock and out of the mill's shadow seemed to me to be my best part, and I could not just leave him to sink or swim on his own. If he had drowned, that part of me would have drowned with him, I think.

Near the end of 1971, Chris went into a Chicken Delight in Portland to get a three-piece Snack Bucket. Just ahead of him, two men started arguing about which one had been first in line. One of them pulled a knife. Chris, who had always been the best of us at making peace, stepped between them and was stabbed in the throat. The man with the knife had spent time in four different institutions; he had been released from Shawshank State Prison only the week before. Chris died almost instantly.

I read about it in the paper—Chris had been finishing his second year of graduate studies. Me, I had been married a year and a half and was teaching high school English. My wife was pregnant and I was trying to write a book. When I read the news item—STUDENT FATALLY STABBED IN PORTLAND RESTAURANT—I told my wife I was going out for a milkshake. I drove out of town, parked, and cried for him. Cried for damn near half an hour, I guess. I couldn't have done that in front of my wife, much as I love her. It would have been pussy.

34

Me?

I'm a writer now, like I said. A lot of critics think what I write is shit. A lot of the time I think they are right . . . but it still freaks me out to put those words, "Freelance Writer," down in the *Occupation* blank of the forms you have to fill out at credit desks and in doctors' offices. My story sounds so much like a fairytale that it's fucking absurd.

I sold the book and it was made into a movie and the movie got good reviews and it was a smash hit besides. This all had happened by the time I was twenty-six. The second book was made into a movie as well, as was the third. I told you—it's fucking absurd. Meantime, my wife doesn't seem to mind having me around the house and we have three kids now. They all seem perfect to me, and most of the time I'm happy.

But like I said, the writing isn't so easy or as much fun as it used to be. The phone rings a lot. Sometimes I get headaches, bad ones, and then I have to go into a dim room and lie down until they go away. The doctors say they aren't true migraines; he called them "stressaches" and told me to slow down. I worry about myself sometimes. What a stupid habit that is . . . and yet I can't quite seem to stop it. And I wonder if there is really any point to what I'm doing, or what I'm supposed to make of a world where a man can get rich playing "let's pretend."

But it's funny how I saw Ace Merrill again. My friends are dead but Ace is alive. I saw him pulling out of the mill parking lot just after the three o'clock whistle the last time I took my kids down home to see my dad.

The '52 Ford had become a '77 Ford station wagon. A faded bumper-sticker said REAGAN/BUSH 1980. His hair was mowed into a crewcut and he'd gotten fat. The sharp, handsome features I remembered were buried in an avalanche of flesh. I had left the kids with Dad long enough to go downtown and get the paper. I was standing on the corner of Main and Carbine and he glanced at me as I waited to cross. There was no sign of recognition on the face of this thirty-two-year-old man who had broken my nose in another dimension of time.

I watched him wheel the Ford wagon into the dirt parking lot beside The Mellow Tiger, get out, hitch at his pants, and walk inside. I could imagine the brief wedge of country-western as he opened the door, the brief sour whiff of Knick and Gansett on draft, the welcoming shouts of the other regulars as he closed the door and placed his large ass on the same stool which had probably held him up for at least three hours every day of his life—except Sundays—since he was twenty-one.

I thought: *So that's what Ace is now.*

I looked to the left, and beyond the mill I could see the Castle River not so wide now but a little cleaner, still flowing under the bridge between Castle Rock and Harlow. The trestle upstream is gone, but the river is still around. So am I.

ACKNOWLEDGMENTS

Grateful acknowledgment is made to the following for permission to reprint copyrighted material.

Beechwood Music Corporation and Castle Music Pty. Limited: Portions of lyrics from "Tie Me Kangaroo Down, Sport," by Rolf Harris. Copyright © Castle Music Pty. Limited, 1960. Assigned to and copyrighted Beechwood Music Corp., 1961 for the United States and Canada. Copyright © Castle Music Pty. Limited for other territories. Used by permission. All rights reserved.

Big Seven Music Corporation: Portions of lyrics from "Party Doll," by Buddy Knox and Jimmy Bowen. Copyright © Big Seven Music Corp., 1956. Portions of lyrics from "Sorry (I Ran All the Way Home)" by Zwirn/Giosasi. Copyright © Big Seven Music Corp., 1959. All rights reserved.

Holt, Rinehart and Winston, Publishers; Jonathan Cape Ltd.; and the Estate of Robert Frost: Two lines from "Mending Wall" from *The Poetry of Robert Frost*, edited by Edward Connery Lathem. Copyright © Holt, Rinehart and Winston, 1930, 1939, 1969. Copyright © Robert Frost, 1958. Copyright © Lesley Frost Ballantine, 1967.

ABOUT THE AUTHOR

Stephen King is the author of more than fifty books, all of them worldwide bestsellers. His recent work includes *The Outsider*; *Sleeping Beauties* (co-written with his son Owen King); the short story collection *The Bazaar of Bad Dreams;* the Bill Hodges Trilogy—*End of Watch*, *Finders Keepers*, and *Mr. Mercedes* (an Edgar Award winner for Best Novel and now an AT&T Audience Network original television series); *Doctor Sleep;* and *Under the Dome*. His novel *11/22/63*—a Hulu original television series event—was named a top ten book of 2011 by the *New York Times Book Review* and won the Los Angeles Times Book Prize for Mystery/Thriller. His epic works The Dark Tower and *It* are the basis for major motion pictures. He is the recipient of the 2018 PEN America Literary Service Award, the 2014 National Medal of Arts, and the 2003 National Book Foundation Medal for Distinguished Contribution to American Letters. He lives in Bangor, Maine, with his wife, novelist Tabitha King.